Books by

Carnal Secrets

Naked Nights

Naked Nights

ISBN # 978-1-78686-086-6

©Copyright Vonna Harper 2016

Cover Art by Posh Gosh ©Copyright 2016

Interior text design by Claire Siemaszkiewicz

Totally Bound Publishing

Carnal Secrets

NAKED NIGHTS

VONNA HARPER

Dedication

To every writer who has ever found the courage to reveal
the deepest parts of themselves.

Chapter One

"She won't stand a chance against you, not with you weighing so much more than she does."

Tray Nix didn't need to be told that. After all, he'd yet to come across a woman who could hold her own against him. The same could be said for ninety-nine percent of the male population. Even though his pro football years were behind him, he still competed in weightlifting events. Just the width of his shoulders was enough to convince most people not to confront him.

"I can see why they arranged to have Carnal harvest her," his companion continued as they waited for the next Copper County race to begin. "The bitch is making fools of the male jockeys here."

By 'they', Carnal Incorporated executive Robert Smith was referring to several heavy betters who couldn't bring themselves to back a female jockey. To them, horse racing was a boys' club. Women could sit in the stands like he and Robert were doing. They could even own horses and work as trainers. However, pitting their racing skills against men, even if the men barely topped one hundred pounds, went against everything their betters believed in.

"They should lay down money on her," Tray suggested. "Seems to me that would end what they consider a problem and turn it into an asset."

Robert chuckled, not that anyone who didn't know the expensively dressed fifty-something man would call it a chuckle. To an outsider, the sound probably came across as a warning, Robert's way of saying he didn't give a damn about anyone's opinion.

The thing was, Tray didn't give a damn what Robert thought and Robert knew it. Their relationship was both complex and simple, two men with very little in common who nevertheless had agreed to work together.

Work? That was one way of putting it.

"I wagered a grand on her." Robert had to press his shoulder against Tray's so they could carry out a private conversation in the crowded stands. "What about you?"

Damn it, betting that much on a weekday ten-furlong race held in a rural county would stand out. Robert had gotten rich too fast helping run Carnal and had lost perspective. If they were going to pull off the harvesting, they had to keep a low profile—at least as low a profile as Tray was capable of. No matter that he was casually dressed in jeans and blue T-shirt, he stood out. He always did.

The eight thoroughbreds in this race were being loaded into the starting gates. From this distance, the animals didn't look that imposing, but he'd been around enough horses to have a healthy respect for them, especially high strung ones. No way would he be on the back of a twelve-hundred-pound beast hellbent on galloping as hard as its heart allowed, especially with other straining beasts all around.

He and Robert had come to Copper County to harvest Marina Stenson, but he'd insisted on observing her in her natural habitat. It wasn't that he gave a damn about the woman herself—years of being a broad-magnet tended to make them all blur together—but her choice of jobs fascinated him.

Some five minutes ago, he'd been standing near the paddock area watching the horses being mounted. Because the jockeys had all worn helmets, at first he hadn't been able to make her out. Then one had turned sideways, giving him a glimpse of breasts under red and black silks. He'd thought the male jockeys might shun her, but they hadn't. *Interesting.*

She'd hoisted herself onto the back of a chestnut mare,

picked up the reins, and leaned over the mare's neck to scratch her between the ears. Watching Marina, he'd wondered what her hands would feel like on him.

Hell, that wasn't what today was about. In time, if things played out the way they were supposed to, she'd learn to accept his hands all over her. Maybe move from tolerating to —

The horses exploded from the starting gate, hooves pounding the packed earth. This was a far cry from the Kentucky Derby, but the crowd's excitement was contagious. Silent, he leaned forward, his gaze locked on the blur of red and black now in second place. Marina's mount ran as if she was trying to beat the ground into submission. Despite that, Marina seemed part of the animal under her, quiet water surrounded by raging rapids. Thanks to his familiarity with horses, it didn't take him long to pick up on a key reason for her success. No matter what was happening around her, Marina remained calm, and that calmness reached her horse. The mare stopped attacking the turf. Her strides lengthened and became smooth. Two furlongs from the end, the duo flowed past the lead horse and cruised to an easy win.

"Damn!" Robert exclaimed. "That's the easiest money I've made all year."

The horses cantered around the track as their riders brought them down from the highs they'd been on. Marina's mare still reminded him of moving water, while Marina now sat straight and proud, looking all around. He could see why someone who hadn't bet on her might see her stance as arrogance. What he didn't understand was how anyone could hate her enough to arrange to have her freedom taken away.

What did he care? By the end of the day, he'd start training Marina Stenson as a sex slave. She'd either be put up for auction at the end or sold before he'd finished working with her. Chances were she'd never sit on horseback again.

Hell, he knew what facing the end of something he loved

felt like.

Chapter Two

Maybe she should have accepted Barker's invitation to buy her a beer, Marina thought as she pulled into the carport next to her small house. After all, Barker had been the first to give her a chance to race and she didn't like thinking about where she'd be without him. Unfortunately, sixty-eight-year-old Barker smelled worse than the fairground's stables. He was also getting hard of hearing and spoke so loudly he gave her a headache. Her other option had been to join several of the jockeys, which was a pretty safe bet because she'd seldom seen one drink more than a single beer. However, by the time she'd gotten away from a reporter, almost everyone had taken off.

The interview questions had been predictable. How did she feel about being a woman in a male-dominated sport? Why had she decided to become a jockey? Was she ever afraid? What did she intend to do once her riding years were over?

She'd had no hesitancy about answering the first two questions but the others were no one's business. Of course fear occasionally factored in, but so far she'd been able to transfer the emotion into determination and split-second decisions. As for her plans for the rest of her life — she had them all right. What she needed was a bankroll to make them come true, which was why she was living in what was little more than a cabin on the five acres she'd bought at auction. All the acreage needed was a water source and fencing to become useful but —

"Enough," she muttered and unlocked the front door. Her fingers still tingled from gripping the reins during the three races she'd ridden in today and her inner thighs ached from holding on. Fortunately, she'd recently put in a new hot water heater and she intended to stand in the shower until it ran out.

Because she needed to check the oil level in her truck, she didn't bother locking the door before tugging off her racing boots. The house was too quiet, eerily empty. Until a month ago she'd shared it with Zero, the mutt she'd found along the side of the road the week she'd turned eighteen. After Zero had died in her arms, she'd stroked his gray muzzle for hours then buried him in the shade of an oak tree. At first she'd been too heartbroken to contemplate having another dog. Then she'd decided that the best way to honor her companion's memory was by giving another stray a home. Unless something came up, she planned to go to the humane society on Wednesday and adopt another mutt.

Smiling, she drew her top over her head and unfastened the confining sports bra on her way to her bedroom. She dropped her discarded clothes on the floor, took a ratty but clean T-shirt and shorts out of her dresser, and entered the bathroom with what she intended to wear after her shower. She leaned against the sink so she could tackle her leggings and the tight breeches that came to just below her knees. That left her with lacy white underwear, her only concession to her feminine side—except for the long, mostly black hair she wrestled into braids on race days. After shimmying out of the bikini, she turned on the water. While waiting for the room to steam, she unbraided her hair and shook her head. *Ah, freedom!*

Yeah, freedom, she acknowledged as she stepped into the small shower. Responsible for nothing and no one except herself and her future dog. Independent. Self-sufficient.

Pitting herself and her mount against the opposition, with her muscles straining and adrenaline flowing, left her more exhilarated at a race's end than before the start. It took hours to come down off the incredible and nerve-wracking high, which meant she'd be wired until long after dark. Even hot water flowing over her did little to quiet the familiar jumpiness, not that she wanted it any other way.

Hell, she wasn't getting any sex these days and frustration contributed to the jumpiness. Fortunately, she knew how to take care of that. Eyes closed, she leaned her back against the shower wall, spread her legs, and slipped her right hand over what her father had called her woman's place. She flicked one nipple then the other, awakening her breasts. Poor Dad. He'd done an admirable job as a single parent right up until his little girl had started to mature sexually. That was when he'd started stammering and shoving sex education books at her.

Maybe they would have gotten past the awkward stage. She'd certainly hoped and expected that would have happened. However, Dad had died shortly before her fifteenth birthday.

No! No thinking about that tonight! She'd made five hundred dollars today. The evening was hers—time for a little self-satisfaction.

One caress. Two. Three. Then more and more strokes along her labia until her knees weakened and hot juices drenched her fingers. Her head fell back, her mouth opened and her nostrils flared. She switched from teasing her taut nipples to pinching them. Pain and something damn good radiated over her size C breasts. Sensation flowed down her middle and met with the sweet energy encompassing her sex.

Well versed in her hot buttons, she conjured up a naked male body. Unlike the men she'd spent her day competing against, the one residing in her mind was heavily muscled with impossibly wide shoulders. Tall and self-confident, he invaded her space and pulled her hands off her body. He made her stand with her arms at her sides as he slipped two fingers past her parted lips. He didn't speak, simply commanded her with a dark look. Even though she wasn't sure she could trust her legs, she remained where he'd ordered and started mouth-fucking his fingers. She repeatedly licked him while staring up into his hooded eyes. The drawing sensation radiated down her neck, spread over her breasts and began a familiar trail to her pussy.

Do what I command you to, his gaze said. *Give me access to all your holes.*

A calloused palm pressed against her mons. Desperate for more, she arched her pelvis toward him. He grunted and shoved more firmly. When she stood her ground, when she opened herself even more to him, he nodded. Fingers closed over her labia, making her moan in anticipation.

Then the intimate invasion shifted, the texture changed, and she reluctantly acknowledged it was just herself after all. She remained with her legs far apart as she withdrew her wet fingers from her mouth and stroked her breasts. The feminine fingers between her legs invaded then filled her opening. It wasn't what she wanted, her fingers were too small, but she'd make do. Fuck herself as the water cooled.

She came, a feathery climax that made her skin burn, followed by lethargy. Feeling both satisfied and still frustrated, she aimed the water at her pussy and washed away the scant discharge. Hopefully she'd be able to sleep. If not, there were always her sex toys.

By the time she'd dried herself, put on shirt and shorts without bothering with underwear and wrapped a towel around her head, she'd mostly convinced herself that she was crazy for thinking she could achieve a teeth-rattling climax on her own. At least it hadn't taken long. Once she'd dried her hair and found her sandals, she'd tend to her truck, starting with adding some oil. While she was at it, she should check the antifreeze and windshield fluid levels. Then, glory be, she'd rustle up something to eat.

The bedroom she'd just stepped into smelled — off. Different. Confused and a little uneasy, she stopped and looked around. Two men stood in the opening between her bedroom and living room. One was huge, an unbelievable mix of height and strength. The other barely registered.

"What the hell are you doing here?" she demanded.

Neither man spoke. Her heart slammed against her chest as if trying to break free. At the same time, her thoughts slowed, focused on the only thing that mattered — survival.

"Leave. Get out of my place."

They continued staring at her. Granted, the window was open enough that she could dive through it but she'd take the screen with her. Adding to the risk, she was barefoot.

She wanted to demand an explanation but didn't because she wouldn't like their response. This was bad, on the brink of a nightmare. If she was going to get out of right now alive, she had to do something.

Not taking her attention off them, she stepped over to her bed and reached under her pillow. She pulled out a utility knife and engaged the blade.

"Interesting," the smaller man said. "I expected a gun."

Her pistol, unfortunately, was still in the truck's glove compartment. She'd never thought she'd need a weapon, but had taken the gun safety course and bought the pistol as insurance. The knife had been her dad's and she'd been sleeping with it ever since he'd gotten sick.

After what seemed like forever, the big man took a forward step. She hadn't wrapped her mind around his size, but at least he no longer shocked her. He simply was what he was, a threat to her existence.

The window. Dive through it while keeping the knife away from her body. Run no matter what happened to her feet. Run while the damn bastards were trying to decide what to do.

She was still trying to convince herself that she stood a chance of getting away when big man took another step.

"Don't!" She sounded more scared than determined. "Damn you, don't!" She pointed the knife at his throat.

He reached for her. Gasping, she scrambled back.

The way he studied her made her wonder if he was concerned she might cut herself. If he was, did that mean they didn't intend to kill her?

"You're not going to get away." His voice put her in mind of rumbling thunder. "Don't make it any harder than it needs to be."

Were they here to kidnap her? That was crazy. No one would pay more than a few bucks for her return.

"Use the Taser," the other man said. "We aren't here to play games."

The way the big man's nostrils flared told her he didn't like being given orders. All right, she wouldn't make that mistake, which left her with one option — the window.

"I want to see what you're made of," Big Man said. "Do you go down without a fight or...?"

Not caring what he was trying to tell her, she jerked back her free arm. Her elbow struck the screen. The screen sagged but didn't pop out. She hit it again, felt it give way.

Holding the knife out from her body, she spun away from Big Man, leaned over, and started to push off with her feet. Before she could dive out of the window, however, powerful hands grabbed her around the waist and yanked her against a solid body.

She screamed and twisted around, slashing wildly. Something struck her wrist, numbing her hand. The knife fell soundlessly to the carpet. She'd just started to kick out when monster-man lifted her off her feet, carried her over to her bed and threw her face-down on it.

"That's how it's done," he announced. She didn't care whether he was talking to her or his companion, just that with his splayed hand pressing against the small of her back, she couldn't push herself off the bed. She managed to turn her head toward him but wished she hadn't because now she was staring at his crotch.

"You could have injured the merchandize," the other man grumbled. "That's why the Taser — "

"I know what I'm doing."

"Not in this you don't. Damn it, you're supposed to follow instructions."

"Yeah, right."

The bed dipped as he climbed onto it, still holding her down. He straddled her hips and brushed her hair off her cheek.

"You're all right? Nothing injured."

Did he expect her to answer, maybe thank him for being so considerate? Not in this lifetime. Much as she needed to get out from under him, she knew better than to wear herself out attempting the impossible.

"I don't want you talking to her," the other man said. "Keep her off-balance."

"Oh she's off-balance all right. Trust me on that. Okay, Marina, time for me to get to work."

He knew her name, which meant what, that they'd been following her? If they had they must know she lived alone.

Her arms had been out from her sides and useless because she couldn't reach back enough to attack him. When the pressure against the small of her back let up, she sucked in a deep breath. He locked his fingers around her wrists. Even though she resisted, he easily crossed one wrist over the other behind her.

"This is why I don't want her out of it," he said. "I want her aware of everything that's happening."

The other man grumbled. His clothes appeared more expensive than her captor's. Maybe that meant Little Man was supposed to be in charge, maybe her captor's superior. Any other time she probably would have laughed at the notion of Big Man allowing anyone to order him to do anything.

Just as he had no intention of letting her up until he was ready.

A shadow at the side of the bed caught her attention. She stared at Little Man, hating him with every fiber of her being.

"What do you want?" her captor asked.

Little Man folded his arms across a silk shirt and stared down at her the way a hunter with a fresh kill would. "I

15

wanted to see if she's trying to fight you."

She wanted to, all right. In fact, it still took every bit of self-control she had in her not to.

"Fortunately no, she isn't."

"What do you mean, fortunately?"

"I've tamed horses. It's a lot harder getting through to the ones that fight than those that understand who's in charge."

Her captor had compared her to a bronc? She wondered if Big Man and she might have an understanding of horses in common — if she lived long enough to find out.

"Tray, I don't want to stay here," the other man said.

"Neither do I. Let me get her ready."

Ready for what? The smaller man had called Tray by name because they weren't concerned she could identify them. Was their intention to take her somewhere, rape then kill her?

For the first time since she'd spotted the men, terror threatened to overwhelm her. She didn't want to die! Not at twenty-four. Her stomach knotted, her heart raced and she had to work at not losing bladder control. Early in her racing career, another horse had collided with the one she'd been riding and both animals had fallen. Even as the ground and flailing hooves had closed in on her, she hadn't been as afraid as she was now.

"She's shaking," Tray announced.

"Good." Little Man leaned down until his face was inches from hers. "Wondering what's going to happen to you, are you? Go on. Conjure up every scenario you're capable of. It'll give you something to do, something that'll contribute to your undoing."

What are you saying?

"You're messing with her mind," Tray said as she willed her muscles to stop jerking.

"You're damn right I am. Does that surprise you?"

"No." Tray drew out the word. He closed one oversized hand over her crossed wrists, which left the other free for what? "I'm just taking note of your techniques."

"My techniques are based on successful methodology. We know what works—and we expect new employees to follow protocol."

When Tray didn't respond, Little Man frowned. She didn't know what to make of the relationship between her captors any more than she could make sense of what she'd heard about technique, methodology and protocol. With her nervous system on overdrive, she was hard-pressed to accept that her world had been turned on end.

Above and behind her, Tray changed position. She was afraid he'd rest all his weight on the backs of her thighs. Instead, suddenly her left arm was free. Before she could think what to do, metal touched her right wrist.

"No!" She tried to jerk her arm free then started bucking. Doing something felt good. Maybe useless but better than surrender.

Despite her struggle, Tray easily locked the cuff around her wrist and pulled up on the metal, increasing the strain on her shoulder.

Sweating, barely able to concentrate on breathing, she forced herself to stop fighting. Tray lowered her tethered arm so her hand again rested on her buttocks. Then he took hold of her left wrist, pulled it back, and handcuffed her. He released her and leaned back. Was that his erection against her crack? She imagined him thrusting his arms above his head like a cowboy who had just roped and thrown a steer.

"It's simple." He placed his hands on her shoulders and lifted her upper body off the bed. "All it takes is a pair of handcuffs and you're under my control."

That and his much larger, stronger body.

And her fear.

He continued pulling up until the strain in her back made her gasp. After holding her like that while she likened herself to a hooked fish, he let go. She fell back onto the bed, smashing her breasts. He didn't have to speak for her to understand his message. He could do whatever he wanted to her and she couldn't do a thing to stop him.

He'd rape her and she'd let him. Get the violation over with. Not let him get off on her resistance.

Unless the instinct for self-preservation made that impossible.

Tray's companion brushed her wet hair away from her face. Instead of leaning close again, he stepped back. His gaze roamed over her, every inch Tray's bulk didn't hide. Even though the smaller man was no longer touching her, she felt as if he was mauling her, invading her private space.

Would she ever have that space back?

His attention settled on her face, and she returned his stare. "Lift her again," he said. "I want to check something."

She thought Tray might object to the command, hoped he would. Instead he vised his fingers over her shoulders and effortlessly hauled her back up. The other man grabbed her T-shirt in front and pulled it up, exposing her hanging breasts. She tried to twist away.

"There isn't much substance to her," Tray said. "Pretty small, are they?"

Instead of immediately answering, the man cupped the breast closest to him and kneaded it. She felt sick.

"Surprisingly," he said, "they aren't. What are they, Marina? C cups?"

Like she'd tell him! Like she'd acknowledge what he was doing!

"Decent knockers," Tray said. "That's good."

"Damn good." Little Man's fingers slid down her breast. Instead of letting it go as she prayed, he caught her nipple between thumb and forefinger and squeezed.

Hissing under her breath, she again tried to twist free. Waves of helplessness washed over her. She'd never felt more alive.

"Hey," Tray said. "I thought you wanted to get out of here."

"I do, but the merchandize is distracting."

Merchandize?

The pain radiating out from her nipple, and now over her

breast, distanced her from the incomprehensible word. The horrible thought that she'd been given a hint of her future seized her. She fought to keep from sobbing but couldn't.

Her tormentor's hold on her nipple tightened, forcing her to clench her teeth to keep from crying again. She was losing this battle, couldn't keep her pain to herself. Just then Tray again let go of her shoulders and she hit the mattress. A moment passed before she realized Tray's action had forced Little Man to let go of her.

"What the hell was that?" he grumbled. "I wasn't through teaching her a lesson."

"I'm going to be her trainer, not you."

Trainer? As in sex slave trainer?

Her world blurred as she recalled a snippet of conversation she'd overhead between a couple of local businessmen who wagered heavily on horse races. She'd been coming out of the women's restroom one afternoon when she'd spotted them standing near the men's restroom.

"I'd love to see her with a collar around her neck," one of them had said. "Naked and on her knees before me."

"Yeah," the other had responded. "A well-trained sex slave."

Chapter Three

Robert was there because that's the way things were run at Carnal, but the older man's presence was the last thing Tray wanted. Sure, he was going to make mistakes on this, his first capture, but as long as he got out of here undetected with his captive unhurt, what did the nuances matter? There wasn't a time clock, let alone a checklist of what had to be done when and in what way.

If it was just him and Marina—he wasn't ready to call her slave—he'd be trying to determine why she wasn't screaming bloody murder. Granted, she lived so far out in the country that no one would hear, but wouldn't she holler anyway?

Instead, she'd pulled out a knife and would have buried it in his neck if he'd given her half a chance.

Hoping to hell Robert wouldn't try to take charge, he climbed off her and stood up. Marina rolled over onto her side, exposing what were indeed size C breasts. They were so damn feminine on her slim, athletic body, larger and riper than the glimpse he'd caught when she'd been getting on her horse had led him to believe. Obviously, she wore something to minimize and constrain them when she was riding. He wondered if her fellow jockeys and others who hung around the county race track knew what she was hiding.

Did the two men who'd wanted her harvested?

She looked down at herself and shuddered. Then she struggled into a sitting position, shaking her upper body until her top slid over those luscious breasts. His fascination with her boobs surprised him. From high school on, members of the opposite sex had thrust their breasts at him. He'd seen some pretty spectacular ones, including dozens with implants. Marina's were natural.

Even without the use of her arms, she reminded him of a predator. There was no surrender in her. He'd demonstrated how easily he could control her, but maybe the lesson hadn't taken. He should've been anticipating teaching this little bitch what she needed to do in order to survive and please men. Instead, he asked himself what the hell he was doing.

For nearly a year now he'd been educating himself in what Carnal Incorporated was about. He understood that the organization's primary function was to supply wealthy and powerful men—and a few women—around the world with well-trained sex slaves. He'd invested in the company and, so far, had no complaints about his dividend checks. At first his involvement had been minimal. Hell, all he'd initially known was that a wealthy alumnus from the university he'd attended had recommended it. That alumnus had gone from dropping a few hints about what went on behind the various Carnal walls to taking him to a party to end all parties. Once he'd recovered from the sight of collared, naked women crouched between splayed male legs, he'd started asking questions. Bit by bit he'd been introduced to the company's inner workings.

Now, maybe, he was about to become an employee.

Shaking off the matter of what had brought him here today, he set his sights on the next step. Getting the slim jockey out of her place wasn't going to be a problem. He could simply throw her over his shoulder and head out the door, but, unless he restrained her legs, he'd have to keep his hands on her for the foreseeable future. She also needed to be gagged.

Before coming here, he'd packed a sports bag with the equipment a senior trainer had recommended. He'd thought the trainer had gone overboard with the variety and amount of restraints, but hadn't argued. Now, as he contemplated what to hobble her with, he realized he liked having options. The trainer had let him in on a not-so-secret secret—that the actual capture was a huge turn-on. Watching Marina watch him pumped up the erection that had sprung to life the moment he'd seen her coming out of the bathroom. As a defensive player, he'd loved staring down at an opponent he'd just knocked to the ground. This was better.

"What are you planning to do?" Robert asked. "You've thought this over?"

He'd always resented coaches who pushed their opinions of how he should do his job on him. It took considerable self-control not to tell Robert to shut the fuck up. Ignoring him, he backtracked, picked up the sports bag and opened it so Marina could see the contents. She blanched and leaned away when he withdrew a long leather strap with a buckle on one end and holes in the other.

"Really?" Robert muttered. "You're sure—"

"Just watch."

As he draped the strap over the back of his neck, he decided to talk to Carnal management about not having to work with Robert anymore. Then Marina bared her teeth and nothing else mattered.

"What do you think you can do? Biting me isn't going to get those cuffs off you."

She glared at him. "You bastard."

"Don't let her get away with that," Robert insisted. "She has to learn—"

"She will, but I don't want to knock all the fight out of her."

"Breaking her down's the whole idea," Robert grumbled. "Don't you get it?"

"Oh I get it." That said, he vowed to stop responding to Robert. He was doing something he'd been fantasizing about for months.

When he leaned over the bed and reached for her, she started to scoot back. Then, to his surprise, she stopped, straightened and glared at him. No matter how many times he'd mentally played out this scene, he hadn't expected this. She was supposed to fight and scream, beg and cry, not immediately give up.

No, she hadn't surrendered. She simply understood how futile resisting was. The question now became whether she'd remember that or whether the instinct for survival would take over.

He grabbed her arm and pulled her toward him, jerking as he did so she lost her balance. As she toppled, he planted his free hand on the back of her neck, spun her in a quarter circle, straightened her legs, and pushed her face into the bedding. He gave a moment's thought to robbing her of oxygen, but he already had an unfair advantage. Besides, he didn't want her in fear of her life.

"Concentrate on your timing," Robert said. "Every move has to be your idea. Don't let her control anything."

Carnal trainers had told him the same thing and he'd taken their advice to heart. Just because the warning had come from Robert was no reason for him to want to do exactly the opposite. He let up the pressure enough to allow her to turn her head and breathe. She stared at his crotch, then angled her gaze so she was looking up at him. Chocolate eyes widened. He wanted to explain why he'd broken into her place but this wasn't the time. First came hammering home the lesson that he was in charge of everything where she was concerned.

Keeping her in place via the neck hold, he snagged the ankle closest to him. He bent her knee until her heel pressed against her ass. That's when he realized he couldn't get hold of the strap this way. As he slowly lifted his hand off her neck, her eyes narrowed.

Keep the slave off balance. Never let her think she knows what's going to happen, or what you're thinking.

The advice had made sense at the time. Now he acknowledged that it was easier said than done. At the same time, he didn't see anything wrong in letting her anticipate.

He pulled the strap off his neck and started to place it on the bed beside her when he changed his mind. Watching her reaction, he trailed the strap down her back. She twitched and panted. Then he slowly guided it down her free leg. She shuddered and tried to slide away. He reversed direction, pushing down on her trapped ankle as he did so she couldn't move. Her panting picked up and her short nails dug into her palms.

"It's beautiful, isn't it," Robert said. "Long as I've been at this, watching a captive's responses still turns me on."

No doubt about it, teasing Marina and seeing what anticipation was doing to her made his cock throb. He didn't want time to matter, wanted to spend the rest of today and all night taking her on one physical journey after another. As a teenager and when he had been in his early twenties, he hadn't given a damn about what his sexual partner was experiencing, but maturity had changed him. He still preferred to focus on his pleasure, but at least he wasn't in such a hurry. When it pleased him to do so, he paid close attention to the woman's responses. He dropped the strap between Marina's legs and pushed up the back of her top and shorts hem so the garments were out of the way. Keeping her leg bent, he slid the strap under her thigh. Using his forearm to prevent her from straightening her leg, he released her ankle, grabbed both ends of the strap, and closed the leather around her thigh and the top of her ankle. He slipped the end through the buckle and tightened it. Once he'd secured the restraint, he tried to slide his finger between the restraint and her flesh. Discovering he couldn't, he stepped back and looked at what he'd done.

The leg away from him was free, not that she was going anywhere. He'd in essence half-hogtied her. Her well-muscled thighs and calves impressed him, but then a jockey needed strong legs. He ran his fingers over both thighs. They were even firmer than he thought they'd be. He'd always been drawn to soft women, yet couldn't help but admire this slight athlete.

Curious to see what she'd do, he patted her ass. She rocked one way and the other. She managed to get onto her side, only to roll back onto her belly.

He patted her ass again. "That's only a taste of what you're going to experience. From now on it's going to be mostly painful."

When he switched to a series of slaps, she struggled to wrestle herself back onto her side. Her low whimper made him smile. The trainers hadn't lied when they'd said how arousing mastering a slave could be. He felt good, damn good. He wasn't sure he'd feel the same way if she'd panicked.

"It's pretty simple." After subjecting each ass cheek to hard swats, he folded his arms across a chest that had convinced more than one man not to try to take him on. "I'm in control."

She closed then opened her eyes. There was no sign of the surrender he'd expected. "Are you going to kill me?" she asked.

"No."

"Damn it," Robert grumbled. "You don't owe her anything."

Robert was wrong. Marina Stenson deserved to know whether she was going to go on living.

"Rape?" She swallowed. "This is all about raping me?"

It wasn't that simple, but even with her dark eyes begging for an explanation, he knew to keep his answer to the minimum.

"I'm not going to rape you."

Her expression clearly said she wanted to believe him, but didn't. Judging by her clenched teeth, she was trying to straighten her hobbled leg. When he'd first seen pictures of her, he'd become horny just thinking about bringing her under his control. It was no longer that simple. For one, he had to make good on his promise not to rape her.

"We're running out of time," Robert said. "The plane's waiting."

She tensed at the word 'plane'. The longer he studied his captive, the less he understood her. The majority of women who'd flitted in and out of his life had gone out of their way to try to please him. His needs always came first. Now he was face to face with one who wanted nothing to do with him.

Fine. Let her think that way for now. He'd teach her to put him before herself.

"I know the plane's there," he told Robert. "Believe me, I've got it."

Outside, the sun slid beneath the horizon. Before long it would be dark. Marina might not have realized it, but she'd never see her home again. He debated apologizing for being such a bastard, then reminded himself of what lay ahead. After months of watching other trainers take their slaves through their paces, his time had come.

As he stood over his captive, he formed a mental picture of what she'd look like with his collar around her neck and his metal clamps squeezing her nipples. She'd be on her knees with her head submissively bowed as she waited for her master's command. Other trainers would acknowledge how well he'd trained her and make bets about how much she'd go for at auction. He'd no longer mess up his mind trying to decide what the hell to do with the rest of his life now that he was too old and beat-up for professional football.

This broad didn't matter. She was simply the means to a considerable paycheck. And a wealth of sexual satisfaction he'd only imagined until now. Instead of him having to wine and dine a potential sexual conquest, this future slave would do everything he wanted her to. And if she resisted—hell, he'd teach her the error of her ways.

Full of himself, he hoisted her over his shoulder and straightened. She fought the arm he'd looped over her waist and her free leg pummeled his chest. He could have tightened his hold on her but didn't because her struggles fed his hard-on.

Robert opened the door and trailed behind him as he carried their captive to the carport. As he waited for Robert to lower the tailgate on her truck, he repeatedly squeezed her buttocks. Damn it, he could hardly wait to get her clothes off.

She cursed, struggling uselessly.

"You aren't going anywhere I don't want you to go, got it?" he told her. "From now on, you belong to me. Believe me, you don't want to make the mistake of screaming."

Expecting her to beg him to let her go, he readied himself to spank her, but she remained silent. Her out-of-control breathing concerned him. Was she going to have a heart attack?

"We need to go back to the house," Robert said. "Make it look as if leaving was her idea."

"I know. Get started. I'll join you."

Robert placed the gym bag in her truck bed then walked away. Tray hoisted her off his shoulder and onto her back near her equipment. When she tried to sit up, he effortlessly rolled her onto her side and held her in place. All those nights of fantasizing about his first capture and here she was, helpless and waiting for his next move.

"I'm not saying where we're going. All you need to know is that the location was chosen for its isolation. You think you have little elbow room here but that's nothing compared to..."

"Why?" she whispered.

"Why? You're potentially valuable, worth a lot more once I'm done with you than you ever could be as a jockey."

He'd designed his response to give her as little information as possible and, judging by how she thrashed under him, he'd accomplished what he'd intended. The trainers he'd talked to had universally cautioned him not to feel sorry for a subject. The less he saw her as a human being, the easier it was to bring her in line. Feeling her strain under his fingers, coupled with her shocked expression, made that difficult. If their roles were reversed, he'd be fighting for his life.

He waited her out. It took several minutes, but finally her head sagged and she stopped trying to get out from under his heavy hand. She was drenched in sweat, her hair sticking to her cheeks and neck while her top clung to her breasts. When he let go of her, she rolled awkwardly onto her belly. Her eyes looked glazed. He hadn't broken her. No way had she given up so soon.

Wondering how much fire burned inside her spent body, he ran his hands under her shorts hem and roughly pinched her ass cheeks.

"No!" She strained to lift herself off the truck bed. Her nails went in search of his hands and he had no doubt she'd tear chunks of skin out of him given half a chance. He stopped trying to pinch her but kept his palms against her buttocks.

"You bastard! Damn it, don't!"

"How are you going to stop me?"

Instead of trying to answer, she turned her head so she was again staring at him. The longer the gaze held, the less he liked it. She was supposed to be subservient, a compliant little slave eager to fulfill his every wish.

An idea—a need even—stirred and he let go of her so he could search through the gym bag. As he dug into the contents, she switched from glaring at him to watching his every move. He held up the sleep mask.

"No." She dug her knees into the floor mat and tried to spin away from him. "Oh please, no."

Unless he was mistaken, her 'please' was the first sign that she'd acknowledged how hopeless her situation was. He told himself he was doing what was necessary to ensure she wouldn't risk hurting herself. At the same time, he was almost sorry to see the fight go out of her.

Not bothering to spell out the obvious, he hauled her over to the tailgate. Even though she kept shaking her head, he placed the sleep mask around her eyes. After securing it, he tried to imagine what being forcefully blinded felt like. He wasn't certain he knew what she was experiencing, but she must feel even more helpless. Until he, her captor, decided to restore that vital sense to her, she'd have no way of anticipating his moves. She couldn't see where they were going.

"It didn't have to be this way," he told her. "If you hadn't tried to stop me from doing this" — he slipped his hands under her shorts — "I might have let you go on seeing."

Her response, if that's what it was, consisted of rapid breaths. She'd stopped trying to get away, making him wonder if she was trying to get into his good graces. Maybe she was so overwhelmed she couldn't remember how to make her muscles work.

If that were the case, he'd give her something to think about.

He pulled her shorts crotch down and to the side, giving his right hand a clear shot at her pussy. He easily found her sex opening. She was dry up there. Acknowledging that his brief manhandling hadn't turned her on took a bite out of his ego until he reminded himself that fear could dry a woman. He moistened his fingers by running them over the sides of her mouth, then pushed one into her.

"No," she whispered. "Please."

Her surrender was music to his ears. He'd bring her down to animal level all right — and enjoy every step of the way. Done right, he could force sexual pleasure on her. That would be her ultimate undoing. Even though he was running out of time and would hear it from Robert, he decided to give her something to think about until they reached their destination.

Wishing he could see more than her hollowed-out cheeks and parted lips, he slowly pumped her channel. Even though he was tempted to give it to her hard, in a matter of seconds, she stopped sucking in air. Her mouth relaxed and her breathing lengthened out. When he again went after saliva to coat her channel, she didn't try to stop him from placing his fingers inside her mouth. She had to taste her sex on him.

He continued to pull her shorts away from her crotch as he repeatedly pumped her soft, and now moist, opening. He no longer had to concern himself with whether she'd try to get away. In fact, judging by how her tethered leg sagged outward and her cuffed hands lay limply on the small of her back, he concluded that her response to being finger-fucked was overriding every other emotion. Her channel heated and filled with slick juice. She angled her free leg outward even more, which made reaching her pussy easier. There was no rhythm to her breathing, no strength left in her helpless body.

Wise in the workings of female sexuality, he occasionally leveled attention on her clit. Every time he touched her there, she shuddered and lifted her ass. Otherwise, she might have been asleep for all the reaction he was getting — except for her flooded channel and out-of-control breathing.

"Killing you is the last thing I'd do." He fell silent as he buried two fingers as deep as they'd go inside her. "You're too valuable the way you are."

"Valuable?"

She spoke so softly he might not have heard if he hadn't been cued into her. He pulled out, swiped her clit, plowed back in.

"Responsive. A horny slut."

"You can't — You can't…"

"Ah, but I am."

His longest romantic relationship had lasted all through his junior year of college and might have continued even longer if he hadn't been drafted. A large part of Rachel's appeal had been her insatiable sex drive. All he'd had to do was give her a seductive look and she had been ready for a round. They hadn't had much in common beyond sex but he hadn't cared. After they'd parted ways, he'd told himself there were other horny bitches somewhere. All he had to do was find them.

Judging by Marina's reactions, she might be one of those. If he was right, training her to be an always available whore should be easy. Giving her up might be another story.

"This is going to be your undoing," he told his now twitching captive. "You'll do anything for a climax, anything. Endure—"

"You work fast."

Tray didn't bother acknowledging Robert. Neither did he have any inclination to hide what he was doing from the other man. In fact, he stepped to the side to improve the view while keeping his fingers in the sweet hot hole.

"I wanted to give her something to think about until we reach—"

"Don't. We don't want the captives to know where they are."

So much for thinking Robert would give him some credit. The damn pompous bastard was still trying to throw his weight around. Instead of pointing out that he hadn't been about to reveal their destination, he wiggled his fingers. He not only smelled the arousal he'd forced on her, he was starting to understand why trainers often blinded their captives. Simply put, they had no choice but to depend on the men who were rebuilding them.

"Are you done?" he asked Robert.

"No. I want you to see what a sweep consists of. Tie her down and I'll give you a demonstration."

He could have pointed out that a blindfolded, cuffed, and one-legged broad didn't need to be tied down, but there was something to be said for increasing her sense of helplessness even more. Besides, if he continued pumping her, she'd probably come, and he wasn't ready for that to happen.

"Give me some rope." He stopped moving his fingers but kept them buried in her. Her pussy muscles tightened around him. Damn but he wanted to get back to learning what made her tick.

For once Robert kept his mouth shut. The other man dug into the sports bag, withdrew a length of white cotton rope and dropped it on her back. He positioned himself for a clearer view of what the shorts' crotch didn't cover. Tray figured Robert was weighing his chances of getting Marina in position for some back door action.

It wasn't going to happen, because this hot little number belonged to him for the foreseeable future.

He debated letting her know they were just getting started, but, as he'd been told, the element of surprise served as a valuable tool. That in mind, he reluctantly withdrew. She turned her head as if trying to see his fingers. So his *abuse* of her sex had made her forget the blindfold.

He picked up the rope and looped it twice around her neck, careful to knot it so it wouldn't tighten. He secured the loose end to one of the truck's tie-downs.

"There." He reached under her belly and unfastened her shorts, then tugged them down, exposing her buttocks. If it wasn't for the leather hobble, he would have stripped her from the waist down. Maybe this was better because she was left to anticipate.

"You going to take pictures?" Robert asked.

Tray reached into his pocket for his cell phone. Obviously, Robert would like to get his hands on her, but knew better than to risk pissing Tray off. In other words, despite Robert's belief that he needed to guide Tray every step of the way today, he understood there were limits to what he could get away with.

Damn right. This future sex slave was his.

He snapped a number of shots that showed her from every angle. The neck rope was so short she couldn't sit up, which meant the odds of someone spotting her were minimal. He supposed he should mentally go over the steps he'd be taking between now and when they reached the west coast facility, but he preferred taking pictures and mulling over the meaning of the word possession.

"Think she's worth the trouble?" Robert asked.

"Hell yes."

"So do I. This one's a winner."

"You hear that?" He patted her naked buttocks. "You're

a winner."

Chapter Four

The men were gone. Marina had heard their footsteps on the gravel walkway leading to her house. In addition, she felt her solitude in her nerve endings — solitude she couldn't do anything about.

She was sweating under the blindfold. No matter how many times she tried to tell herself that discomfort was why she couldn't dismiss not being able to see, it wasn't the truth. Her captor must have known how vital vision was to her, which was why he'd robbed her of that precious ability. He'd handed her dramatic proof of how easily he could control her, and yet, not being able to use her hands or stand was nothing compared to blindness. They could return and she wouldn't know. They might point a gun at her temple and she wouldn't have any idea what they had in mind until the half-second before a bullet tore through her brain.

No, they weren't going to kill her. At least not yet. But maybe if she tried to call for help — not that anyone would hear.

She kicked out, then sobbed under her breath when she couldn't straighten her leg. The leather strap dug into her flesh but hadn't cut off her circulation. Tray hadn't needed to hobble her. Surely he knew she couldn't outrun him with her arms secured behind her.

Even though she hadn't bothered with briefs, the shorts had seemed adequate when she'd put them on. Back then she'd believed she'd be spending the night alone. All she'd needed was a minimum of clothes on the remote chance one of her so-called neighbors dropped by.

Instead, Tray and another man had invaded her world.

The muscles in her arms and shoulders burned, prompting her to stop trying to lift her hands off her buttocks. She wasn't going anywhere. Couldn't even see.

Judging by the cooling air on her exposed ass cheeks, she guessed the sun had set. The approaching night didn't matter as much as what she'd learned at Tray's hands.

He could turn her on.

Moaning, she tried to brush the sleep mask against the truck's floor. Tray had done more than lock her in darkness — he'd played with her body, slid his fingers into her sex hole and forced arousal from her.

She didn't want to respond to his forceful touch, damn it! That was the last thing she wanted. If he knew how little it took to turn her on, he might use his knowledge against her.

What did she mean *might?* Her body had given up its secrets to the big man who'd captured her.

Even more unsettling, she remembered every touch.

A crunching sound jerked her back to reality. The men were returning. She tried to curl up, only to stop and chide herself for attempting the impossible. If she was going to survive this, she had to make Tray believe she was immune to his sexual touches.

Somehow.

"That's why we target loners," Little Man said. "Bitches with a network of friends and family are more trouble than they're worth."

"I get it," Tray responded. "How many potential slaves does Carnal reject for that reason?"

"Hmm. I can't give you a percentage, but it's considerable."

Something heavy thudded on the truck bed. She tried to imagine what of her belongings her captors had decided to take with them, but wasn't sure it mattered. One thing she was certain of, they were intent on severing her ties with the world she knew.

The only thing she didn't know was why.

Or did she?

"What happens now?" Tray asked. "Does Carnal let those who nominated her know she's been taken?"

"Sometimes. Sometimes not. I'm not sure how this is going to play out."

"They'll figure it out before long."

Desperate for more pieces of the nightmare puzzle, she waited for the men to continue. Instead, a hand smacked her left ass cheek.

"Get used to this, slave," Little Man said. "It's just a taste of what you're going to experience."

"Hey." Tray sounded angry. "What'd you do that for?"

"Damn it, do I have to spell it out?" He slapped her again. "This gives her something to think about."

"I already have." Someone, she guessed it was Tray, pulled up on her cuffs so she felt the strain throughout her upper body. "This is enough for now."

"You haven't gotten to the punishment part. That's where the real education takes place."

Tray kept her arms in the air. "Believe me, I understand. I just thought—"

"How about we talk about it once we're on our way?"

In other words, they didn't want her hearing. Tray let go of her wrists. Little Man slapped her a third time, then one of them unfastened the strap. Before she could straighten her leg, someone did it for her. She kicked out when one of her captors started to wrap the leather around her ankles. Her sad attempt at defiance earned her a series of stinging slaps on her buttocks, and she forced herself to stop squirming. She fought tears as her ankles were bound together.

Why is this happening? She longed to ask but she didn't want to know.

One of them rolled her onto her side. Something that tasted like rubber was shoved against her teeth. Once more she fought but again lost the battle. The moment she reluctantly opened her mouth, a ball was rammed into it. The ball was fastened in place via straps that went around the back of her head.

She couldn't yell for help.

Was completely at their mercy.

She barely reacted when someone pulled her shorts down until they reached the rope around her ankle. This was someone else's nightmare. It couldn't be happening to her.

The truck rocked, and when she smelled canvas, she surmised they'd stretched a tarp over the truck bed so no one would see her. A voiceless prisoner being taken where?

She whimpered when the engine started, then forced herself to fall silent because otherwise her fear might have been her undoing. She was being driven away from the only place she'd been able to call her own. She'd be used for sexual purposes. The idea of being forced into prostitution made her sick to her stomach until she told herself she could probably escape.

Before long they left the dirt driveway and turned onto the quiet county road. The truck had turned left, which meant the freeway might be her captors' destination. They could go west or east or hook up with a north–south freeway. She'd gassed up this morning, which meant they could go hundreds of miles before having to stop. Unless she could spit out the gag or pound her feet against the truck bed, they'd be in and out of a gas station without anyone knowing about the trussed-up woman under the tarp.

How long until dark? Probably less than a half hour. Her captors might decide to get something to eat but they'd carefully planned her capture, which meant they wouldn't do anything that put them at risk. They might give her something to drink or let her go to the bathroom, but she couldn't imagine them caring whether she got hungry.

Where were they taking her, and what did they plan to do with her once they reached their destination?

How long before anyone realized she was missing? As a self-employed jockey without an agent, she was free to ride for any owner who approached her. This year she'd been able to pick and choose and, although she'd committed herself for the entire racing season, she wasn't sure the owners would come looking for her. They might simply complain about how unreliable she'd become and select a replacement. She had friends, of course, but no one she considered particularly close. Currently, there was no man in her life.

She'd long been aware of her solitary nature and had occasionally tried to be more outgoing, but it hadn't been a good fit. Until his death, her father had been her best friend. She didn't know how to replace him, or if she wanted to.

Now, when it was too late, she realized that in some respects she'd set herself up for what had happened.

The tarp started flapping and the tires made a whining sound. She'd been so lost in thought that she could only guess they were heading west. Determined to remain in the here and now, she drew mental images of where she figured they were. Then the truck slowed and angled to the right. Had they gotten off the freeway? Maybe they'd already reached the north-south thoroughfare. The tires started their high-pitched whine again and the tarp sounded as if the wind was attacking it. All she knew for sure was that they were putting her world behind her. She was being spirited away to where?

* * * *

Marina couldn't say how long they'd been traveling when the truck stopped. Maybe an hour, maybe longer. Much as she'd loathed being taken where she didn't want to go, believing they'd reached their destination was even more unnerving. Fresh air entered her nostrils, making her guess the tarp had been removed or at least drawn back. Even though the neck rope was loose enough for her to turn over, she didn't try because that would've put too much weight on her arms. Besides, she couldn't see anything.

"That worked slick," Little Man said. "The package has barely moved. Let's get her transferred. You want to take her to pee or — "

"She's my responsibility. I'll handle it."

The tightness around her ankles ended. She tried to separate her legs, but her shorts stopped her. Even though she thought she'd prepared for it, she shivered when one of the men tugged them off. She was still trying to make her peace with half nudity when she realized he was doing something to the rope around her neck. As he hoisted her into a sitting position, she was caught between relief at this small amount of freedom and the feel of rope against the back of her neck and trailing between her breasts.

"Let's go." Tray grabbed her ankles and dragged her along the truck bed toward him. Despite her efforts, she lost her balance and banged the back of her head. He continued to haul her until her legs dangled over the tailgate.

"All right, slave, sit up."

Slave? Surely he didn't mean —

"Did you hear me?" He slapped her thighs. "Sit up."

As she reluctantly obeyed him, she wondered at the change in his attitude. Earlier he'd treated her as if she meant something to him, while now it was as if she was an animal that had displeased him. Maybe Little Man had lectured Tray on how to treat a — oh, God, a slave.

Tray took hold of her upper arms and pulled her up and forward. Afraid she'd fall, she scooted to the end of the tailgate and reached out with her toes. One moment she was in space, the next her feet landed on gravel. With Tray hauling on her right arm, she had no choice but to try to follow him. The gravel cut into her feet.

"Useless bitch," he muttered.

With that, he lifted her and threw her over his shoulder. She could have tried kicking — if she'd had a death wish. As he effortlessly carried her, she fought not to choke on the realization that she was at his mercy. He could carry her for hours, set her down, and walk away, leave her blind, silent, disoriented, and without use of her arms. They weren't in a jungle but might as well have been.

She had to get in his good graces, somehow.

Unless she couldn't force herself to.

A familiar and disgusting smell assaulted her. She surmised they were near an outhouse. A door squeaked open, and he stood her up. She shuddered at the feel of the public facility's floor under her bare feet and didn't dare move for fear she'd bump into the toilet seat. When Tray turned her around, despite what she'd warned herself about angering her captor, she couldn't help but resist. He grumbled something she couldn't make out and pushed her back. Her naked ass landed on hard plastic.

"Get it done," he ordered.

Tray was watching her, listening for the sound of urine. Hard as it was to focus on her bladder, she had no choice if she didn't want to risk wetting herself later. She finished what he'd brought her in here to accomplish, then tried to squeeze more liquid out of herself. To her disgust, he pushed down on the back of her head until she was leaning way over and, reaching past her ass cheeks, wiped her.

His responsibility.

His slave.

She was so horrified by what had just happened that she barely paid attention as he hauled her to her feet and dragged her back outside. She nearly lost her balance stepping down. She collided with him, and he roughly jerked her upright. The outhouse door clanged shut. A moment later she heard it squeak open again. As awareness of the space around her increased, she realized he'd left her alone so he could use the facilities. If only she could see!

But she couldn't because that was what her captor wanted.

It was cooler than it had been when they'd taken her from her house. She had no idea where they were, and only the faintest hint of their plans for her.

"Good." His comment was accompanied by the door's complaints. "You at least know enough to stay where you belong."

He effortlessly hoisted her back onto his shoulder, and

because it didn't make any difference, she didn't attempt to hold her head up. She reluctantly likened herself to a just-shot deer on its way to being gutted.

A warm hand rested on her naked buttocks and a broad finger prodded between her ass cheeks. Holding her breath, she waited to see what he'd subject her to, but instead of claiming her pussy like before, he rested his finger against her bung hole. He made no attempt to push past the puckered opening, but he could if he wanted to.

What would Tray do to her? Subject her to?

Maybe it was not having use of her hands and being locked in silent darkness, but an image formed in her mind. She lay naked and spread-eagled on Tray's bed. Her wrists were chained to the metal headboard while more chains held her ankles where Tray had placed them. She was gagged, but the blindfold had been removed so she saw him enter the room.

This man who'd laid claim to her body walked over to the bed and stood looking down at her. He was fully clothed but had unzipped his fly so his cock jutted out from his remarkable physique. He held a dildo in one hand, nipple clamps in the other.

"Today's toys, slave. Time to make you scream."

"I've transferred everything," Little Man said. The mental image shattered. "And I rubbed down everything we touched. Soon as I take a piss, we can take off."

"No rush," Tray said. "I can handle her."

Little Man chuckled. "Yeah, you sure can."

At the crunching sound, she surmised Little Man was walking away. By transferring everything, did he mean they'd be getting into a different vehicle?

Instead of putting her down, Tray started rubbing her buttocks. The contact was gentle, almost reassuring. As he ran his finger between her cheeks and lightly scratched her ass hole, she stayed relaxed. It was as if her body belonged to someone else. She was here simply to experience knowing hands. This powerful man wanted her. She'd become important to him. And because she had, he wouldn't hurt her.

The only thing he'd do was take away her will.

Alarmed by how easily she'd surrendered self-determination, she tightened her butt cheeks.

He pulled out and slapped her ass. "You aren't getting rid of me that easy." He slapped her repeatedly while she squirmed uselessly. "Bad decision on your part. Corrective action on mine, got it?"

Embarrassed by the spanking he was subjecting her to, she tried to apologize but either he couldn't understand what she was saying or he chose to ignore her. Finally he laid her on carpeting. Despite her stinging buttocks, she chanced stretching her legs. Judging by the metal her feet encountered, she guessed she was in the back of a SUV. This had been planned! Part of their scheme for her. Being helpless in her own truck had been bad enough, but this was even worse. Screaming into the gag, she started thrashing.

"What the hell?" Tray said. "Haven't you learned your lesson?"

Short Man chuckled. "Don't worry about it. The bitches always panic. Tie her down before she hurts herself."

The SUV sagged under Tray's weight as he climbed in next to her. He forced her onto her back and straddled her. Unable to stop herself, she kept trying to buck him off her. Her arms were being smashed but it didn't matter. She'd had it, couldn't take any more.

"Here," Short Man said. "You can let her fight later, but now isn't the time."

Tray again looped the strap around her ankles. However, instead of securing her legs next to each other like before, he placed one leg over the other before cinching the strap tight. Her pussy was caught, clamped, her sex lips pressing against each other. She gasped and tried to convince herself to stop struggling.

"Here's this," Little Man said. "You might want to use it."

"Hmm. Yeah, I think I do."

More leather circled her thighs. She cursed and fought to wiggle out from under Tray, but he easily tightened that strap. Resisting had only increased her bondage.

Tray lifted off her and tried to run the side of his hand between her legs near her crotch. "That did the job. I just wish I'd plugged her first so she'd have that to think about."

"Next time. She'll get the message."

No, she wouldn't! Just because he'd trapped her sex was no reason for—

Tray rolled her onto her belly and swatted her buttocks, distracting her from the lie she'd been trying to convince herself of. As he exited the back of the SUV she tried to tell herself that at least he hadn't retied the neck rope, but it didn't matter.

They had her.

Chapter Five

Tray had never needed eight hours of sleep, but he was dragging by the time the private Carnal plane landed at the seaside airstrip shortly after daylight. He and Robert had each driven during the three hours it had taken to get to where the plane had been waiting. After transferring their captive to the plane, they'd had to cool their heels for a couple more hours so they could take off in the middle of the night. Even though their seats reclined, he hadn't been able to sleep because he kept thinking about the half-naked, trussed-up package on the floor behind him. He'd done it. Pulled off his first capture.

Done something he wasn't sure he wanted to talk about.

Robert had played a vital role in getting her here, and his lecture about how captives should be seen as possessions and not human beings had reminded Tray of everything he'd been told during his indoctrination. If not for Robert, he might still be deluding himself into thinking this was destiny.

He and Marina Stenson hadn't been brought together for the perfect master–slave relationship. She wasn't a natural submissive any more than he'd been born with a trainer's whip in his hand. Truth was, she'd caught the negative attention of the wrong people and he'd been chosen to turn her into his first sex slave. He'd train her. She'd be sold. He'd move onto his next conquest.

"I'm starving," Robert said when the plane stopped moving. "What if we grab something to eat while they get her settled in?"

His stomach rumbled at the thought of breakfast, but

watching Marina try to wrap her mind around what was happening held more appeal. "Go," he said. "I'm staying here."

Robert laughed. "I figured you'd say that. I was once where you are now, hot and horny and barely able to wait to get started. Just don't forget she's a valuable piece of merchandize, nothing else."

Tray didn't bother responding. Soon after Robert took off, two men wearing jeans and collared shirts with the initials CI in red on them climbed in. They acknowledged Tray with a nod then entered the cargo area. They grabbed Marina by her shoulders and feet, and she started struggling. He came too close to telling them not to hurt her before remembering Robert's warning about her being merchandize. They hauled her over to the exit and the larger man started down the stairs. The other pushed Marina out feet first. The one on the ground grabbed the strap around her ankles and used his handhold to guide her down. If the man still in the plane hadn't had hold of her shoulders, she would have tumbled out.

After the three were out of the plane, he stepped into early morning sunshine. Marina's handlers were carrying her by her shoulders and ankles to a waiting SUV. He couldn't stop staring at her naked ass.

He'd done this. Taken away her freedom.

His hard-on returned. He had to forcefully remind himself that it was vital for Carnal to see him as a competent trainer and not some oversexed boy.

"You want her in the dungeon or a training room?" the man holding her ankles asked.

"A training room," he said, because the dark dungeon with its cages set him on edge. No way could he work in there. "I want to get started as soon as possible."

"I don't blame you." The man plopped her buttocks onto the SUV tailgate and cupped his palm around what he could of her mons. "Damn, but I love this job."

Tray clenched his fingers. "Don't."

The man withdrew his hand. "Sorry, man. I was just getting a sample. Some trainers pass the merchandize around. Obviously you don't."

Maybe, eventually, he'd offer Marina to those who worked at the facility, but not now. One reason he'd been drawn to the job was because he needed to prove, maybe just to himself, that just because his playing days were behind him, was no reason to plop his ass in a chair. He could have gone into business or climbed onboard the speaking circuit, even tried his hand at acting, but none of those possibilities appealed. He still needed physical activity, and the thrill that came with pitting himself against an opponent.

Granted, there wasn't much of a physical matchup between Marina and himself, but there was more than one kind of competition. He intended to win this one.

Once Marina was in the back, he climbed into the passenger seat. The handlers explained that once they were done with this run up to the facility, they'd return to the plane for the equipment and overnight bags he and Robert had brought with them. They'd also grab Marina's belongings and place them in Tray's room. As they started up the short climb to the sprawling facility that overlooked the Pacific Ocean, Tray tried to remember what of her things Robert had selected. There was her laptop, purse, and a few personal items, including some clothes so it would appear as if she intended to be gone for a while. Her cell phone was at the bottom of the outhouse. They'd left her truck with the keys in it in a low income part of the next town north of where she lived. Chances were someone was already driving it and getting their fingerprints all over it.

The coastal Carnal facility had once belonged to an investment company that had used the eight-bedroom monstrosity to wine and dine high rollers. The company had gone bankrupt during the recession and Carnal had picked it up for pennies on the dollar. Since then, the basement-wine cellar had been converted into a dungeon. Half of the bedrooms now served as residences for trainers while the others had been modified for training purposes. There was a large kitchen and a great room, complete with fireplace adjacent to a cedar deck. A forty-step walkway led down to the isolated beach surrounded by vegetation made lush by the Pacific Northwest climate.

"How'd you get along with Robert?" the man behind the wheel asked.

"What do you mean?"

The man shrugged. "I've been working here for going on three years and he still treats me as if I don't know shit."

"There were some rocky moments, but he knows what he's doing." He glanced behind him and noticed that Marina was shivering. It was warm in the SUV, so fear must be responsible.

"Will he be overseeing you?"

"I'm not sure."

"Good luck if he is. Of course, you're more intimidating than most, so maybe he'll treat you like an equal."

If Robert rode him too hard, he'd tell him to back off. On the other hand, like he'd just said, Robert knew the ropes when it came to slave training. He'd put up with enough hard-ass coaches to know how it was done.

They pulled up at the back of the facility. Tray got out and opened the back door. "We'll take care of her," the driver assured him. "Unless you want."

"I want her to see what she's up against." After reaching in, he spun her around so he could get his hands on the sleep mask. She was a delectable package all right, with a bit of mystery thrown in, because she was still wearing her top. Despite her rough night, her long, thick hair felt like silk. The rope around her neck stood in sharp contrast to her tan body. He started to unhook the mask, only to stop and reach into his pocket for his cell phone. He took several pictures of the helplessly bound package before unfastening the mask. The moment it was off, he aimed the phone at her face. He snapped three shots as she blinked repeatedly. Her eyes were darker than he remembered, full of disbelief, horror and hatred. The hatred fascinated him.

"You're here," he said unnecessarily. "Get used to it."

He stepped back so the handlers could take over, then nearly objected when they freed her legs. It belatedly dawned on him that they wanted her to have to walk to her prison. Her legs nearly gave out as they stood her upright. After a moment, she flexed and straightened her legs, glaring at him the whole time. Saliva trailed from the gag and some had dried on her top.

Curious about her reaction, he reached behind her head and loosened the gag. She didn't wait to see what he had in mind but spat it out. Her head up, she licked her lips.

"Interesting," the shorter man said. "I thought she'd start screaming. There's a lot of that around here."

Tray shook his head. "So far, she's been pretty quiet."

"That'll change once you start working on her."

Thinking Marina might beg for an explanation, he continued his perusal of her, but she only studied her captors in turn. He'd figured her emotions would be simple with fear front and center but, unless he was wrong, defiance was wrapped in with her loathing of him. His job included wrenching defiance and hatred out of her on the way to subservience. Right now he wasn't sure how he felt about that.

He took hold of the neck rope and started hauling her around to the metal side door used by slaves and trainers. At first she resisted, but it didn't take her long to figure out how little chance she had of fighting him. Something about dragging her behind him put the final pieces of the puzzle together for him. His little slave in training was finally here. From now on he'd be in control in ways he hadn't been when football management could buy, sell or release him. He was no longer a well-paid but disposable athlete. He was in charge of another human being.

The slave door was constantly monitored, so, after ringing the buzzer, he waited for the door to swing their way. The two who'd come for him and his captive might have already been back in the SUV in preparation for retrieving what remained in the plane. Except for when he'd taken her to the outhouse, this was the first time he'd been alone with his captive.

She'd back-stepped after he stopped leading her. As a consequence, the rope from his hand to her neck was tight and she reminded him of a reluctant dog or about-to-bolt horse. Her nostrils were flared, her eyes wide and mouth parted. Seeing her tremble, he nearly told her what to expect, then remembered yet another of Robert's warnings which was to always keep the slave off balance and guessing.

The door opened and he stepped into a windowless office. A fifty-something woman sat behind a teak desk with video monitors all around. Everyone called her Mrs. Johnson. All he knew for sure was that no one wanted to get on her bad side, in large part because she was the facility's financial officer. He'd never seen anything approaching a sense of humor from her, and she always carried a switch. He'd watched her use it on more than one slave. She was good with it, damn good. And ruthless.

"I have her paperwork." Mrs. Johnson removed several pages from the printer and slapped them down on the desk near where he stood. "Robert said he'd sign them, but as the slave's primary, that's your responsibility."

He switched the lead to his left hand and leaned over so he could read the document. The rope connecting him to his captive trembled. The document contained a lot of legal verbiage about his financial responsibility should the subject be injured, followed by a lengthy confidentiality statement. In essence, Carnal operatives would take him out if he so much as said a word to law enforcement. The statement wasn't necessary because Robert and others had made it clear that certain powerful members of the legal and political systems throughout the country availed themselves of Carnal's services.

"Do I still have room three?" he asked as he signed.

"Let me look." Mrs. Johnson tapped her keyboard. "Yes,

it's ready for you. I had to replace a camera, but it's been tested." Head cocked, she studied Marina, who was trying to take in the entire room. "She a jock?"

"In a way. She's a jockey."

Mrs. Johnson snorted. "*Was* a jockey. Not every potential owner wants a slave with muscles."

I do. Surprised by his thought, he nevertheless shrugged. "They prefer someone soft? Where's the challenge in that?"

"Spoken like an athlete. Look, I had reservations about letting you become a member of the *family* not because I wasn't certain you could do the job, but because I'm not sure you know your strength. It'll be interesting to see what you do with her."

Mrs. Johnson didn't intimidate him. The less he had to do with her the better, and if she came near Marina with her whip, he'd stop her and deal with the consequences. As he studied his half-naked captive, he wondered if she fully understood how many cards were stacked against her. Not only was she a prisoner in a facility designed to contain captives, the few free women here were part of the power structure. They didn't see the slaves as their equals in any way. In essence, Carnal existed as its own country with its own rules and ways of enforcing those rules.

Mrs. Johnson jerked her head at a camera on a tripod to the left of her desk. "Get her over there and get the hell rid of her clothes."

Marina sucked in a noisy breath. Determined to prove he knew what he was doing, he grabbed her hair and hauled her in front of the camera. When Mrs. Johnson handed him a pair of scissors, he slit Marina's top from hem to neckline. He lifted the ruined garment off her breasts, then positioned himself behind her and pulled back on her arms so her breasts thrust forward.

"Nice knockers," Mrs. Johnson said. "Bigger than I thought they'd be." She pushed a button. The camera made clicking sounds. "Turn her around."

Marina continued to noisily suck in air while he did as

Mrs. Johnson had ordered. Until this moment, he'd been aware of how tired he was, but suddenly it didn't matter. He felt alive in ways he hadn't since his playing days. He slid the top down her arms, fisted her hair, and forced her to slowly turn her back to the camera. He didn't wait for another command but bent her forward and kicked her legs apart. The camera swept down her spine and over her buttocks before settling on her now exposed pussy.

"Get rid of that bush. Do you know whether she's ever taken a cock up her ass?"

"No, I don't."

"Hmm. Small as she is, she's going to have trouble accommodating you. I'll send in an assortment of butt plugs. Make sure she wears them."

Marina whimpered and tried to straighten. Seeing other slaves locked into contraptions that kept their holes plugged was one thing. Subjecting Marina to the same thing was another. Maybe he wasn't cut out for this gig after all.

The hell I'm not.

Damn it, he had to stop thinking of her as Marina Stenson. From now on she was simply a slave in training. That would do the trick. The owners of the three teams he'd played for hadn't felt a moment of remorse when they'd given him his well-compensated walking papers. That had been business. So was today.

He hauled her upright. "You need anything else?" he asked Mrs. Johnson.

"Not now. I'll be in later." The corners of her mouth opened in a poor imitation of a smile. "Have fun."

Chapter Six

The cell—Marina didn't know what else to call it—wasn't much larger than her own bedroom, but the only resemblance was that both had a bed. The space Tray had just pushed her into did nothing to calm her nerves. She didn't dare speak for fear she'd start to beg. Pride was all she had left.

She was naked except for the fabric hanging off her cuffed wrists. Being able to see and having the gag out of her mouth felt wonderful, as did the loss of the straps that had been around her ankles for so long. Even though she should've been trying to make sense of what had happened when they'd come inside, her mind kept closing down. The mental numbness wasn't that different from what she experienced right before a race. During those seconds as her mount strained to start running, only becoming one with the horse mattered.

This wasn't the same as perching on a thoroughbred's back. For one, nothing about right now had been her idea.

Tray closed the door behind her, positioned her in the middle of the room and stepped back. She'd whimpered when he'd forced her to lean over so that horrible woman could take pictures of her private parts, but she wouldn't make that sound again.

At least she prayed she wouldn't.

Neither would she acknowledge her helplessness, she vowed, as she took in this new space. In addition to the bed with its metal head and footboards, there were two chairs. One appeared comfortable while the other—oh, God, the other looked like a torture device. It was made of wood and metal and had been welded to the floor. Instead of a seat, there was a cutout. A metal post extended from the floor to just beneath where the seat should have been.

Despite her frantic attempt to keep her mind blank, she got it. Dildos could and undoubtedly would be attached to the post. Leather straps were fixed to the chair arms and legs. Other straps dangling from the chair back were designed to go around her neck. Once in it she'd be unable to move. The only other piece of furniture was a tall, narrow dresser with a half-dozen drawers. Maybe they held clothes, maybe something else.

A closed door opposite the bed momentarily distracted her. Then she forced herself to acknowledge the rings and chains attached to the walls. Other chains hung from the ceiling. Cameras had been mounted in every corner.

There was a window, small and so high she wouldn't be able to see out. It was open and the glorious scent of the sea drifted in. Knowing she could smell but not see the ocean nearly brought her to her knees.

Please don't do this to me! I haven't done anything to deserve this. Why do you hate me so much?

He opened the door opposite the bed, revealing a large bathroom complete with glass shower. "We'll be sharing this with another trainer and slave. First order of business, getting you on the toilet."

Trainer. Slave. The words crashed into each other in her mind and shattered. This wasn't happening! She was having a horrible nightmare.

Then Tray yanked on the neck rope while jabbing a finger at the bathroom and her desperate lie died. Between fear and thirst she could barely swallow. She wasn't sure how she managed to walk and not shuffle. Eyes downcast, she sat on the toilet. At least the bathroom smelled like cleaning products, unlike last night. Her bladder immediately let go. She steeled herself for him to wipe her again. Instead, he reached into his pocket and withdrew a key.

"Stand up."

Urine dribbled down the inside of her left leg as she obeyed. When he lifted her bound hands and unlocked the cuffs, she caught sight of a camera near the ceiling. Metal now dangled from her left wrist. Her arms fell to her sides and the burning sensation in her shoulders made her gasp.

"That's what I figured would happen," he said as he yanked off her ruined top. It fell to the floor and he kicked it into a corner.

When he started rubbing her shoulders, she did all she could do not to cry out, but before long, circulation was restored enough that she could flex her fingers.

"I've been thinking about this for a while." He re-cuffed her hands in front, then lifted them and knotted the neck rope to the cuff chain so her hands were anchored under her chin. "Now it's time to get you cleaned up."

As he removed his clothes, she backed away as far as she could. It did no good because she still felt his heat. Ignoring her, he turned on the shower. That done, he faced her. He'd been imposing earlier, but that was nothing compared to what she was seeing now. He didn't exactly have a six-pack, but only a thin layer of fat lay over his hard-muscled body. His shoulders and chest were massive, his neck thick. Auburn hair dusted his chest and what little he had in the way of a belly. More reddish hair framed his erection, as if challenging her to ignore the message behind his hard-on. Of course she couldn't, any more than she could pretend he wasn't now staring at her as if he owned her.

His brows were thick and dark, and he needed a shave. She'd spent much of the past few years competing against men barely any taller than her. Maybe that was why she couldn't wrap her mind around her captor's size and undeniable strength. The bathroom wasn't large enough for the two of them, and yet obviously he intended to share the shower with her.

A plea for mercy pressed against her throat. At the same time, an unwanted tingle whispered to life between her legs. Tray was all sex, commanding sex.

And she knew or thought she knew what he wanted with her.

"Take a look at it." He cradled his cock and aimed it at her crotch. "Before long you'll be begging for it. On your knees and begging."

He'd glanced at the camera before speaking. Did that mean he was directing his comment at someone other than her, maybe playing to the unseen audience?

"Where are we?" She licked her dry lips. "On the west coast, but where?"

"That's none of your concern. All right." He jerked his head at the steaming shower. "Get in."

Her fingers kept twitching. Every time she tried to move her arms, the rope pressed against the back of her neck. Helpless. So helpless.

Defeated and yet relieved, because this way she should be able to get a little water in her mouth, she did as her captor commanded. As warm water washed over her sweat and urine-stained body, she reluctantly acknowledged she'd obeyed this man who'd said he was going to train her. She was like a green-broke horse, skittish and half-wild, unable to escape.

He stepped in after her and closed the shower door behind him. Then he pulled her back against him and looped an arm around her arms and she knew. He'd do whatever he wanted to her. She had to get used to it.

Effortlessly keeping her sealed to his harsh body with his cock between them, he maneuvered her under the shower. She lowered her head to keep water out of her eyes and nose, stuck out her tongue and tried to lap moisture into her mouth. He hadn't just turned her into a green-broke horse, she was acting like an animal, dealing with her thirst in the only way she could.

"Don't move," he commanded. "Got it?"

Where could she go? Besides, she'd just discovered that if she lifted her head a little, water ran into her mouth.

He soaped a washcloth and rubbed it over her, starting

with her head. What did she care what he used to clean her hair? She kept her eyes and mouth closed until he reached her neck, then kept her head under the stream until she no longer felt soap on her cheeks. Hard as she tried to disconnect herself from her body, she couldn't stop thinking about what he was doing. The hours of dark, silent, helpless fear and no sleep faded from her consciousness. This was here. Now. Sensation.

Still behind her, he soaped her shoulders, arms, and hands. Then he lifted one elbow at a time and repeatedly ran the washcloth over her breasts. He lingered on her nipples, rubbing them until her knees weakened and her veins heated. She leaned against him, eyes barely open and mouth sagging, lost in her body's responses. Any moment he might hurt her but until, or if, that happened, pleasure would continue to seep into her. She'd put terror behind her.

"What happened to your tension?" His breath warmed the top of her head. "Any more relaxed and I'll have to hold you up."

He was teasing her, challenging her to resist, but how could she? Her breasts had become so sensitive she was barely aware of the rest of her body. Her nipples were hard knots, the rest of her breasts hot and tingling. All these years of celebrating her independence, and in less than twenty-four hours she'd become something else.

Something compliant.

"Turn around," he ordered as he pushed her away from him. "Face me."

Sensual lethargy fled, leaving her tense and as afraid of herself as she was of him. He'd shoved her into the corner. As a result, when she spun on her heels, her buttocks pressed against the tile walls. He cocked his head and added more soap to the cloth. "Belly first, then I'm going to clean your pussy."

She'd been giving herself showers since she was three — shortly before her mother died — and yet what Tray had just said made perfect sense. After all, she belonged to him.

No I don't, she insisted as he spread soap over her belly and hips. This was just a momentary thing, a bit of insanity until she — she what?

Was this what her existence would be like from now on? Tray would do whatever he pleased to her and she'd accept? His handling would so confuse her she wouldn't be able to think past it?

"Legs apart, slave. There's work to be done there."

Slave. There was that word again.

"What's going to happen to me?" she asked as the cloth glided over her labia. This wasn't her! She wouldn't—

"Whatever your master wants to happen."

Master!

"Please tell me what this is about. It can't — I can't—"

He slapped her cheek, knocking her head to the side. "Shut the fuck up. And stick out that cunt of yours."

What a fool she'd been to think he had any humanity in him. She'd seen horse handlers who relied on whips and intimidation to control their animals. She just hadn't allowed herself to accept that Tray would be like them until she had no choice.

"You want a repeat lesson?" He splayed his hand over her belly and pressed her into the corner. "Get your cunt out there."

She hated exposing her sex to him but did as he'd commanded. She readied herself for a harsh scrubbing. Instead, after covering her pussy in soap, he dropped the cloth and started stroking her there with his fingers. Tense as she was, she was grateful for every moment of kindness he granted her. He might switch, of course, and become Master, but she needed memories like this to keep from losing her mind.

She longed for gentle touches, craved the reminder that she was a sexually mature woman. Keeping her sex accessible to him, she closed her eyes. He'd immobilized her arms but hadn't lashed her legs together because he'd been anticipating having access to her pussy.

Yes, that's what it was, her pussy, a base word to accompany a primal action. A stranger taking liberties because he could. He separated her labia and worked a slick finger into her channel. Her inner muscles tightened around the invasion.

"That's right. Let me know how much you want me there."

She didn't. This was simply her body responding to a touch, surrender because resistance was impossible.

He pushed deeper, withdrew a little, probed even more. Her legs started shaking.

"Give it to me, slave. Turn your cunt over to your master."

He wasn't saying this, he couldn't be. Instead, they were lovers playing a kinky game. She'd suggested they pretend he'd captured her. After messing around with the notion of bondage for a while, they'd climb into bed and fuck. Her pelvis wasn't really thrusting toward a big and powerful stranger while he plundered —

"Well, hello," a strange male voice said. "No one told me I'd be sharing the bathroom today."

Tray pulled out of her and planted her back under the spray. She couldn't see. "Hell," he said, "I didn't hear you come in."

The other man chuckled. "You were occupied. How long are you and the bitch going to be in here?"

"Nearly done. She was dirty from the trip here."

"Got it. You want us to come back?"

Tray didn't immediately answer. "No. My slave needs to see yours."

Another chuckle from that stranger compelled her to chance getting out from under the spray. She thought Tray might punish her for disobeying. Instead, he turned off the shower and stepped out. Water streaming off his massive tan back and pale buttocks distracted her. He was everything the word 'powerful' symbolized.

"Don't just stand there." Tray grabbed a towel and started

drying himself. "Get the hell out of there."

Something about his harsh tone made her wonder if he was determined to prove himself to the other man. As she joined him on the plush white bath rug, she forced herself to acknowledge the newcomer. This man wasn't nearly as big or imposing as Tray, but he carried himself with confidence. His head was shaved, and judging by the way his nose canted to the right, she guessed it had been broken. He was dressed all in black, complete with sturdy boots that seemed out of place here.

Then, wishing she didn't have to, she focused on the woman with him. Like her, the woman was naked. Her hands were behind her, her blonde hair caught in a crude ponytail. She looked up at Marina then went back to staring at her small feet.

A leather collar with a metal ring at her throat partly obscured her neck. Two slender chains stretched from the collar to rings through her nipples, lifting her breasts. Horrified, Marina fought not to cry out.

"That's right." The other man caught one of the chains between thumb and forefinger and tugged so the breast was lifted even higher. The woman moaned and shook her head. "She's decorated."

"Decorated?" Tray dropped his towel and lifted Marina's arms, exposing her breasts. "That's not what I'd call it. More like permanently augmented."

"Semantics." The man let go of the chain and tugged on the other. "Whatever label you want to put on these little things, they keep her in line, don't they, slave?"

"Yes, Master," the woman muttered.

She sounded so disheartened that Marina longed to hug her. Tray was still holding her elbows up and giving the stranger a clear view of her breasts. No way was this anything except two dominant men jockeying for position. Would Tray pierce her breasts and push rings through them?

What hell had she been forced into?

59

"The facilities are all yours," Tray said. "I need to let my trainee eat and sleep. Otherwise she isn't going to be able to focus on her lessons."

"Hmm." The other man jerked on the chain, forcing his prisoner to stumble toward the shower. "Keep her hungry and sleep deprived. It'll make training her easier."

"It probably would." Tray released her elbows, grabbed her sopping hair and started pulling her, head down, toward the room they'd been in before coming here. "Any other tips you have, let me know."

"Carnal management wouldn't have brought you onboard if they hadn't figured you were a quick study. You'll do fine."

Fine? Doing what?

Chapter Seven

Tray studied the woman stretched out on the narrow bed. He'd spread-eagled her face up but had left her bonds loose so her limbs weren't being stressed. He'd debated keeping the neck rope on, but the leather around her wrists and ankles made that overkill. She hadn't said a word when he'd picked her up and deposited her on the bed, hadn't tried to prevent him from spreading her legs and anchoring them down. As he'd restrained her arms, she'd turned her head away and closed her eyes. If not for her taut muscles and the way she kept holding her breath, he might have been fooled into believing she didn't care what had happened to her.

Right now she was asleep, sometimes limp with a serene expression, sometimes shuddering and clenching her fists. It had taken her the better part of an hour to nod off. During that time, she'd alternated between studying him sprawled in the easy chair and staring at the wall. Not that he intended to tell her, but he had his reasons for handling things the way he had. For one, he wanted his hunger to mirror hers for a while, so he'd understand a bit of what she was experiencing. The other reason went deeper, and hopefully brought her closer to understanding his total control over her. He wanted her to wonder what he was thinking as he stared at her naked, helpless body, to imagine him doing things to her she couldn't stop. She needed to try to anticipate his next movement, to take in the made-for-restraint room and imagine how it would be used against her.

Most of all, he needed her to start emotionally turning

herself over to him.

She'd stirred when he'd left to eat about an hour ago and briefly opened her eyes the moment he'd returned. She hadn't spoken. Neither had he. Although there weren't any clocks in the room he guessed she'd been asleep for going on three hours, which meant it was time to get started.

When he leaned forward and clapped his hands, her eyes sprang open and she fixed her attention on him. Earlier, he'd found a change of clothes for him outside the door, undoubtedly Mrs. Johnson's attention to detail. He'd approved of the tight black pullover because it defined his muscles. Since it was hard for him to find jeans that fitted over his thick thighs, he wore sweats whenever possible. Like the shirt, the sweats were black. He probably looked like a nightmare to his trainee.

"We're working toward a common goal," he told her once he stood over her. "You're going to be taught to be a sex slave, at my hands."

Her eyes widened even more and she tugged on her bonds, which made her breasts jiggle. His groin tightened. Damn it, not having sex until she was ready was going to be damn hard. It didn't have to be like this, of course, because she was his to do what he wanted to, but his parents hadn't raised him to rape women.

They hadn't raised him for this either.

Hell, his old man hadn't been on hand for anything.

"The course will take however long it takes," he continued. Right now wasn't about reconciling his new career with his so-called moral code. Maybe it never would be. "There'll be tests along the way. If you fail one, I'll repeat the lesson." He planted his hands over her breasts and shook his head, stopping her from trying to shrink away. "You'll hate many things about the classes, but this place is well designed to restrain and contain reluctant students, so you have no choice."

While watching her sleep, he'd had plenty of time to plan what he intended to do today, but eager as he was to get started, he simply remained beside her with her ample breasts under his palms. Her heartbeat vibrated through his fingers. She made him think of spring, that time of year when a frosty night could kill fragile new growth. Keeping her alive and physically healthy while molding her was going to be a delicate operation.

"The school's premise is simple." He positioned his thumbs and forefingers around her nipples and closed down a little. "At the core, pain and pleasure are the same. They're both intense sensations. The majority of us prefer pleasure, but when there's no choice we adapt to pain. Otherwise, we wouldn't survive. We more than accept it. We embrace discomfort because it proves we're alive — and because we always hold out hope that pleasure still exists."

Judging by her expression, she didn't grasp what he was saying. That was probably because her dread of what he intended to do made concentrating next to impossible. That was all right. He had the perfect demonstration planned.

At least he hoped it would be.

"Pretty sensitive here, aren't you?" He tightened his hold on her hard nubs. "You're feeling this all the way through you."

"Don't, please. Oh please don't."

Fear had forced the plea from her, not that he blamed her. If he'd been tied down the way she was, he'd be fighting the restraints like a mad man.

"Oh, but I have to. Otherwise you'll never have value."

Her head whipped from side to side, whether because she was trying to deal with her discomfort or because she was trying to make sense of what he'd just told her didn't matter. Part of a Carnal trainer's goal was to keep a trainee off balance. The more a future slave had to depend on her trainer to give her world order, the more subservient she became.

"There won't be a test today." He drew her breasts toward him, watching for a change of expression. She was holding on, but just barely. "I'm certain that's a relief to you. The lesson about to begin is as basic as they get. I'm introducing you to a marriage of the good and bad. Don't worry about trying to keep them separate." He didn't add that if he did his job as he hoped he was capable of, she wouldn't be able to.

As he released her nipples, her hands stayed fisted and her muscles trembled.

He walked over to the dresser and opened the top drawer. There might be times she wasn't restrained in here, which meant he'd have to remember to lock the drawers. It wouldn't do for her to get her hands on anything she could turn into a weapon. He hefted three sets of nipple clamps, then selected the lightest one. After palming it and putting his hand behind him so she couldn't see, he returned to her. Her attention locked on his arm.

"It won't do me any good to beg you to let me go, will it?" She swallowed. "Damn it, I don't want to, but I might not be able to stop myself."

Suddenly off balance, he bought time by turning his attention to the nearest camera. Wasn't she supposed to struggle and cry? As long as he saw her as nothing more than a female body he could immerse himself in the experience. If she was trying to play with his emotions — no, scared as she was, he couldn't imagine her deliberately doing that.

"This is about teaching your body the meaning of inescapable pain." He held up the clamps by the chain. "What you say doesn't matter. Only experiencing does."

Her expression said she understood what the clamps were for. He supposed she could have engaged in bondage play in her private life, but the file he'd been given on her had led him to conclude she was strictly vanilla, and that only occasionally.

"These won't cut the flesh," he started then stopped. Every move he made would be closely scrutinized and analyzed. Doubtless, he'd be warned not to say or do anything the slave might construe as empathy.

"You're at my mercy, my whim, my sadistic nature, if

that's how you choose to see it." He positioned his left hand around her breast and brought his fingers together. As he one-handedly spread the clamp's teeth, she dug her heels into the bed and twisted away. She had to know her attempt at escape wouldn't change anything, but he didn't blame her for trying. He squeezed, pushing her nipple up even more. Her muscles stood out as she fought her bondage, and he waited her out. When she started to settle down, he positioned the clamp around her nipple and eased it into place.

"Ah! Oh, God, ah!"

Fighting an emotion he wanted no part of, he listened to her pant. She had a look of sick anticipation as she waited for him to finish the awful job. Instead of immediately imprisoning her other nipple, he held back. No one had warned him that he'd feel like this, a little disgusted with himself. She continued to breathe faster than he thought possible, making him conclude this was her way of dealing with pain. If she kept it up much longer she'd hyperventilate, then where would she be?

Maybe unconscious and unable to participate. Getting him out of something he didn't want after all.

No, damn it! He wasn't a quitter, never had been.

"Anticipation." Hoping no one saw his expression, he closed his hand around her other breast. "Sometimes anticipation is wonderful. Other times it's the pits. We both know which this is." There. He'd said what was expected of him.

"Don't talk," she whispered. "Don't— I don't want to listen to you."

Not at all the response he'd expected. Maybe he should ask Robert for tips on how to best deal with her—and himself. No, that wasn't his way.

As he'd done with the first one, he drew out the moment of nipple capture. He split his attention between the clamp's alignment and her expression, because he didn't want to damage her. She was no longer looking at him, which made his task easier. It wasn't until he released the clamp that he realized she'd been staring at the camera—maybe daring whoever was watching to acknowledge what she was being forced to endure.

Her breath hissed.

"I'm all that matters." He tugged on the chain. "Only you and I exist."

Her gaze swung to him. She was still afraid and trying to deal with having her nipples pinched, but, unless he was mistaken, she'd already accepted what was happening.

Knowing he had to push her, he jiggled the chain. Her nostrils flared. "That's what I want, your full attention. The circulation's being cut off here." Careful not to risk ripping off the clamps, he pulled some more. It was getting easier, marginally. "What sucks the most is you can't do anything about it."

"I know, damn it."

Struck by her attempt to communicate with him, he let go of the chain and started running his nails over the top sides of both breasts. Every pass left faint white lines that contrasted with her full flesh. He wasn't sure what that felt like, maybe a blending of positive and negative sensations.

"Not going to kill me." She clenched her teeth. "I know you aren't going to kill me. I'll hang—hang on to that. Let it—"

Acting without thought, he slapped her, cutting her off. A moment ago her eyes had appeared glazed, but he'd brought her back to the here and now.

"You're not going away again, got it?" He slapped her a second time, leaving a red mark on her tan cheek. Hopefully she couldn't guess he was trying to get through to himself, not her. "From now on what I say and do is the only thing you give a damn about, get it?" He slipped his forefinger under the chain and pulled up until she arched her back.

Do what's expected of you, like you have countless times before.

"Get this through your head. Your survival depends on your ability to please me and whoever I sell you to."

"Sell?"

Yes. "Did I give you permission to speak?"

Confusion now shared space with the pain in her expression. "Permission?"

"You know who's in charge. I've changed my mind. There's going to be a test after all." He was being watched and judged. His performance needed to rock, to convince.

On the brink of spelling things out, he looked down at his prisoner while continuing to draw the chain and her breasts toward him. He'd wait her out, make her beg so Robert and the others would have no doubt of his ability to do his job. He sure as hell wouldn't allow himself to get hung up again with questions of what made him think he had the right. Shit happened. This was a prime example. Only it wasn't that simple.

"What test?" The question ended with a hiss, and she remained arched.

He leaned down so their faces were inches apart. She was an opponent, a member of the opposing team. "I'm your master. Call me Master. Otherwise, this is going to get worse." He tugged.

"Ah! Oh shit."

"Who am I?"

Tears welled. "Don't make me—"

"Who am I?"

"Master," she sobbed. "You're my master."

Instead of the sense of power he expected, he wished he was anywhere except there. Aware of the all-seeing cameras, he shoved the impulse into submission and kept the tension going on her breasts.

Her eyes glittered and her features contorted as she fought to accept what she couldn't change. He'd broken several bones during his playing years, the most severe in his lower right leg three years ago. Writhing on the turf with a bone sticking through his flesh had hurt the worst by far. Surely what she was feeling wasn't on the same level, but maybe there wasn't enough difference between the helpless sensations. "There," he said as he let up on the tension. "That wasn't so hard. I won't give you an 'A' because your heart wasn't in it, but you've passed the first test." *Hopefully, so have I.* "Reward time."

Chapter Eight

She hadn't done anything to deserve this. She was responsible and law-abiding. Her life had had its ups and downs, including a couple of major ones, but she'd been proud of her ability to cope. These days, she supported herself doing something she loved and was good at. One day she'd have a husband and children, but in the meantime she'd pay her taxes, vote and give unwanted dogs a home.

Why was she in this nightmare?

The man who'd insisted she call him Master had returned to the dresser she already dreaded. He hadn't removed the nipple clamps and pain throbbed through her. Desperate as she was to ask how long he intended to keep her like this, she vowed not to beg to be set free.

When he turned toward her, she saw what reminded her of the kind of electric vibrator she occasionally used on sore muscles, except this one was shaped like a huge cock. He plugged it in and turned it on. The head pulsed. Was he going to place it on her breasts, maybe hold it against the clamps?

I don't want this! For mercy's sake, don't put me through this.

Instead of giving voice to her fear, however, she forced herself to move beyond her bondage. Just because he'd imprisoned her body didn't mean he'd done the same to her spirit. "This can't be what it takes for you to feel like a man," she threw at him. She'd deal with the consequences of her words later. "You're everything the word 'male' stands for. Women— Women must fall all over themselves trying to get your attention, so why are you—"

"Shut up!" He slapped her cheek hard enough to knock

her head to the side. "What motivates me is none of your damn business."

As she waited for the stinging to subside, she warned herself not to say anything that might make him angry. The problem was, she didn't know what would set him off and if she didn't speak, he'd think he'd won.

He hadn't. She wouldn't let him.

Somehow.

He grabbed her chin and turned her head toward him. "Listen to me, slave, because I'm only going to explain this once. Any time you think you have something worth saying you'll start by asking for permission. Let me hear you say it."

Go to hell, you bastard. "Master." She spat out the word. "May I speak?"

"No, you may not."

His expression changed, became introspective, making her wonder what he was thinking. Then he jerked his head at the chain resting between her aching breasts. "To state the obvious, the clamps are an example of what constitutes pain here. Maybe I should leave you alone so you can fully, and at length, experience the sensation, but I'm going to have to do something about feeding you so you'll stay strong. With that in mind, I've decided to move right onto bringing pleasure into the equation. That, in part, is why you need to remain quiet, so you can focus."

She hated how he threw complex sentences at her when she'd become basic and primal, a tethered creature with an empty belly and clamped nipples. If it took calling him Master to get through this she would. Only she would know she was really calling him a bastard.

He turned off the vibrator and rubbed it over the cheek he'd slapped. "You live alone and haven't dated recently, which means it's just you and your sexual needs. The private detective said you don't pick up men and don't screw around."

A private detective had been watching her? She felt sick.

70

"Maybe you don't have much of a sex drive, but I don't think so and even if that's true, Carnal has tested ways of turning slaves into nymphs. This" — he activated the vibrator — "never fails to do the job."

The tool shook her face. Despite herself, she tried to turn from it, but he kept her where he wanted by tightening his hold on her chin. Already, she was less aware of the discomfort in her breasts.

"That's a good slave. Embrace this lesson. The more you accept it, the more pleasure you'll experience."

Pleasure? Wondering if she dared believe him, she willed herself to look at him. After a few seconds, he released her chin and ran the vibrator down the side of her neck. From there he moved to her arms, down her sides, circled her belly. Anticipating the shuddering sensation on her breasts was driving her crazy. At the same time, she relaxed a little.

This man hadn't just taken away her clothes and tethered her to a strange bed in a strange house, he might have a touch of humanity in him. Maybe he cared about her.

Maybe.

"You can speak now," he said, "as long as you tell me what I want to hear. Do you appreciate this? It's better than setting fire to your nipples."

"Yes," she whispered. "It is."

"No." He sounded more disappointed than angry. "What are you supposed to say?" He didn't give her time to respond before picking up the chain and drawing both breasts away from her body. As if that wasn't bad enough, he ran the vibrator from the inside of one breast to the other. Her breasts were indeed on fire, sparking as if he'd touched them with electricity.

"I don't — please, what do you want me to — Master! You're my master."

Looking sober, he nodded. "Good. I'm going to give you a bit of a break by not requiring you to say anything else. The only thing you need to do is experience."

As if she had a choice. The harsh upward pull on her nipples hurt and she'd have given anything to have it end. At the same time, the quivering felt good. He'd trapped her in a world filled with good and bad, desire and dread, and she couldn't think how to make it end. Maybe she didn't want it to.

"Think about this, slave. Pull sensation deep inside you and acknowledge that your master is responsible for everything you experience. If you please me, you'll receive pleasure. If you anger me — well, I don't have to spell it out."

"No," she managed. "You don't, Master."

He smiled. At least she thought he had because as off-balance as she was, she couldn't be sure about anything.

"You'll stumble during your training." He let go of the chain and silenced the vibrator. "That's to be expected. What you must understand is that I'm demanding. I won't tolerate failure."

Maybe he wanted her to tell him she would do her best to please him, but she couldn't force out the words. She still felt as if she was being shaken and, if anything, the burning in her nipples was becoming worse.

"I'm more than your teacher, of course. I'm your master. Your body belongs to me."

That was a warning, she had no doubt of it. Dreading his next move, she kept her attention locked on his hands. Horses did the same once they figured out what part of an owner's body controlled everything. Master — was she already thinking him as that? — would feed or starve her, beat her or — or what?

"An example of what I mean by body ownership." He once again activated the vibrator and ran it from her neck to the space between her gaping legs. Before she could give silent thanks because at least that was behind her, he touched her clit.

She shuddered and lifted her head trying to see.

"I've trained a few horses," he said. "My experience isn't as extensive as yours, but I think you'll agree that the way to work with herd animals is to present yourself as the dominant member of the herd." He slid the vibrator over one pussy lip, then the other. "That's what I am, slave. The dominant one, which makes you the submissive."

She wasn't, damn it! No way would she submit to this bastard — unless she had no choice.

He lifted the tool so she could see it, then positioned it near her mouth. "Guess where it's going. I haven't checked to see whether you're wet down there, but I strongly suggest you moisten this so it'll go in easier."

"It's too big."

"No it isn't. In fact, I had it made to duplicate my cock's dimensions. Look at it this way. You're going to get advance indication of what fucking me is going to feel like."

Why did she keep saying something when she didn't want to communicate with him? Desperate to erect a barrier between them, she faced the wall on the opposite side of the bed from where he stood. How long would it be before he let her up?

"Have it your way," he said. "But if it hurts going in, that's on you."

And if the vibrator caused her pain, it would make this so-called lesson even harder to endure. Even though she hated herself for giving in so easily, she swung her head toward him and stuck out her tongue. He pressed the now-quiet tool against her lips. She opened her mouth wide and tried not to think as she let him have his way. She repeatedly moistened the rubber-tasting head, gagging as she did.

When he withdrew the vibrator, she started at the slick surface. He was going to fuck her with it.

"Is that what capturing me is about?" She didn't care whether he punished her. "You get off on torturing me?"

"Playing with you, not torture. I've long wondered how far I could push a woman and now I'm going to find out, but it's a lot more than that."

Hoping he wouldn't spell out more than she could handle, she tried to close her eyes. Unfortunately, that reminded her of when he'd robbed her of the ability to see, and she opened them in time to see his attention shift from her face to her groin.

Get it over with. Let him have his way. Then he'll let me eat.

She again lifted her head, but his hand was in the way. The moment the shaking sensation settled over her pussy, she filled her lungs and tried to find a place for her mind to go. The ocean — the ocean —

"Oh," he said, "there's something I haven't told you. So far, you've only experienced the lowest setting."

The shaking intensified, scaring and exciting her. As unwanted pleasure took hold, she acknowledged she'd suspected this would happen all along, but had been denying the possibility. She started rocking her hips and pulling on the ankle restraints, but of course she couldn't get away.

Her pussy came to life, slipped into a place she couldn't control.

"To point out the obvious, I'm strong. I can keep this against your pussy far longer than you can handle it."

Her nerves under and around the vibrator head started to quiver. All too soon they'd short-circuit, taking her mind with them.

"Why?" She hated her pleading tone. "Master, why?"

He didn't immediately answer. "I don't need to explain."

As the violent shaking continued, she again fought to take her mind somewhere else. She saw waves, but instead of lapping against the shore, they were attacking it. She tightened her inner muscles, but that only made things worse. He was right, he could *torture* her until she became crazy.

Crazy for a climax.

A new fear assaulted her. What if his intention wasn't just to demonstrate how easy it was for him to make her climax but to force one explosion after another out of her? She might pass out from over-stimulation, but eventually she'd come to and he'd still be here. Waiting to break her apart again.

"Please. Please."

"Please, you're ready for the next step? That must be what you mean."

The vibrations slowed. Praying for the impossible, she waited for him to turn it off. Instead, he used his fingers to draw her sex lips away from her opening while holding the vibrator head against the space between her pussy and anus. Shiver after shiver assaulted her.

"Going in."

Her body fought to repulse the vibrator. She sobbed in frustration, dread and anticipation as his tool filled her. He kept it up until she was stuffed, the shaking reaching her core.

"There you go. Daddy's home. Take a minute to wrap your mind around this new development while I remind you of the pain element."

She barely noticed when he slapped her left breast. Then he did the same to the right. The blows weren't particularly hard, but her trapped nipples screamed a silent protest. Keeping the vibrator lodged inside her, he repeatedly slapped her breasts. Pain latched onto them. She grunted.

"Doesn't sound as if you're having much fun. Let's see if I can do something about that."

The beast in her pussy kicked into a higher gear. She hadn't begun to accept the new assault when he started pulling up on the chain.

Her breasts were in agony, her pussy alive with hot need. She'd nearly drowned once, had gone down for the proverbial third time. Strangely, as her lungs had filled, she'd stopped being terrified and had started to feel calm. This was different and yet the same. In neither case did she have any control over what was happening.

"If you remember one thing about this," he said, "remember that I can force you to experience everything I want you to. Your time of freedom is behind you. From now on I call the shots."

The vibrator all but exploded, sending never-ending

sparks through her. Her battery-run dildos were nothing compared to this. Most frightening, she couldn't turn it off. It wouldn't run down. Master could control her like this until she died.

She rolled her head about and yanked at her bonds. The pulling on her breasts seemed to be growing worse, not that she was in any position to judge. From the waist down she felt as if she'd stepped into an earthquake. Desperate to get away, she dug her heels into the bed and tried to scoot back, but of course Master kept after her.

Good. Even with all that helpless dread, it felt good.

"You're sweating, slave. Your eyes keep rolling back. Can you hear yourself?"

Hear? What did that matter when a monster had taken charge of her sex? Master angled the vibrator one way then the other so the head sent shards of heat throughout her channel.

"Please, oh, please."

"Please what? Oh, I know. You're saying you want more."

She froze at the thought that the vibrator might have an even higher speed, but that wasn't what he had in mind. As he drew the beast out of her, her inner walls stopped screaming. Instead of relief, however, she felt lonely.

He pulled her breasts down then up, twisted the chain so they were drawn together.

"Please, Master. I can't—"

"Yes, you can. It'll be worth it."

She'd opened her mouth, maybe to beg some more, when he pressed the vibrator against her clit. Just like that she climaxed.

A climax? No, a series of sensual peaks that kept going higher. Wonderful as they felt, she was becoming more incredibly sensitive there. Her clit burned and throbbed. Her mind splintered.

Garbled sounds burst from her. Sweat streamed. She started to drool.

"Dance for me, slave. Understand."

Understand what? The only thing she knew was that she was exploding. Falling apart.

"I won't need to break you because you're doing it to yourself. Go on." The vibrations ended only to start again. "Try to convince me I don't own you."

He did and would continue to. She couldn't go anywhere, couldn't protect herself from the now awful climaxes. Barely aware of what she was doing, she stared slack-jawed at her captor while her body continued to jerk.

He stared back, his gaze intense, as if he was trying to read her mind.

Chapter Nine

"That's one way of doing it," Robert said. "I must say it was entertaining."

Tray turned from the video they'd been watching so he could study Robert's expression. He felt as if he'd just played a double overtime game, spent. Even though Robert continued to lightly hold the glass of expensive scotch, his jaw muscles occasionally clenched.

"Entertaining you wasn't why I did what I did."

"What was your motivation?" Robert went back to watching Marina, who now lay on her side on the bed, restrained only by the chain on her left ankle. "What do you want to ultimately accomplish?"

Tray sipped on his drink, hoping liquor would calm his libido, which remained as high as it had been when he'd been working the slave. "I intend to turn her into a moneymaker for both Carnal and me."

"Is that all?"

Determined not to fall into a trap, if that was Robert's intention, he shrugged. When the two of them had started watching the slave, she'd looked as if she was out of it, but she'd started moving her arms and legs. How much of what he'd put her through did she remember? It couldn't be as much as he did.

"Why don't *you* tell me what you think my motivation is?"

Robert chuckled. "Good response. You're proving that not all jocks are dumb. I'm asking questions I don't believe you can answer at this point. Don't worry about it. Most new trainers go through a period of self-assessment. We expect it. What I want you to consider is whether you get more out of seeing her suffer or watching her climax."

He hadn't expected the question but now that it had been asked, he took it seriously. As he mulled over what he'd experienced during her first session, he kept his attention fixed on the female who was on her way to becoming a slave. She sat up and started fingering the chain anchoring her to the bed.

"I'm not sure. I've never experienced either so — "

"Oh, I'm certain you've given pleasure to a lot of women."

He hoped he had. Most of them had acted like it. "Those times weren't in the same universe as what happened today."

"You didn't have any sex partners who wanted to fool around with bondage play?"

If Robert's intention was to goad him, he was getting into dangerous territory. "That's not what I'm talking about and you should know it. There's a big difference between the kind of play I've done and forcing something inside someone who can't stop me."

"Yes, there is. So back to my question, what turned you on the most, experimenting with the nipple clamps or hearing her scream in pleasure?"

His trainee stood and walked as far from the bed as she could. Judging by the way she was looking at the bathroom, he figured she either had to pee or was wishing she could take a shower. After tugging on the chain, she sat on the side of the bed and started running her palms over her breasts. Indentations from the clamps still showed and she was probably working circulation back into her boobs.

"Are you surprised by what you're seeing?" Robert asked. "Maybe you thought she wouldn't have recovered so soon."

It depended on what Robert meant by *recover*. He debated pointing out that she was barely touching herself, but that might lead to a discussion of semantics, something he wasn't interested in. Besides, he didn't dare forget that

Robert's job was to judge his competency as a slave trainer. Hell, maybe he should ask, because he sure as hell couldn't figure himself out.

"I was turned on," he admitted. *And sometimes disgusted with myself.* "There's something about being able to do anything I want to a subject as long as I don't damage her."

"I'm glad you made that clarification. Damaged goods are worthless to Carnal. Go on."

Marina, his slave in training, had slumped over. Wondering if she might be on the brink of passing out, he frowned. Then her right hand left her breast and settled between her legs.

"I didn't expect that," he muttered.

"Why not?"

She started to stroke herself, her fingers barely touching still-swollen flesh. "I guess I thought she'd be so disgusted by what I put her through she'd be trying to pretend that part of her didn't exist."

Robert chuckled and sipped. "Long as I've been at this job, you'd think I'd understand what makes females tick, but I don't have a pussy. My conclusion, their brains and clits get all mixed up."

Earlier he'd hinted he'd make it impossible for her to differentiate between pain and pleasure. Maybe he should have added that she'd also be unable to distinguish between what her mind needed and her clit wanted and therein lay his greatest power.

"I don't think there is a difference in what I experienced during the first session," he told Robert as he stood up. "I got off on everything I did to her." *Liar.*

The older man smiled. For the first time, his eyes sparkled. "That's what I wanted to hear. So what's up next?"

Once again his attention shifted to the video, where his captive still lightly stroked her sex. Self-doubt no longer concerned him. "Lesson number two."

"Pleasure and pain?"

Think. What's expected? "Maybe more discomfort and less

80

relief."

"Why's that?"

"So she understands who's in charge." He didn't add that seeing her pleasuring herself instead of him doing it to her didn't feel right. She was his. No way did or would she ever have any influence over him.

She was property, a project, a future paycheck. Hopefully.

Chapter Ten

Marina started at the sound of the door opening. When the big man in black entered, she jerked on the ankle chain, followed by cursing herself for letting him see her try to escape. She wouldn't be surprised if he'd watched her, but after what she'd been through, she had to determine if everything down there was still intact. To her surprise, she'd been able to stimulate herself when she thought her sex would be done in. Maybe she could keep her unexpected responsiveness private. That could become her secret, one of very few things he didn't know about her.

Maybe.

"On your knees," he ordered from his position by the door. "From now on that's the position you'll assume every time you see me."

Like hell.

But she was helpless, she reluctantly admitted as she got off the bed. For the time being she had no choice but to submit to his stupid need to dominate her. Then she allowed herself to acknowledge the paper bag in one hand, a water bottle in the other. Did that mean he'd brought her something to eat?

"You shouldn't have taken so long. You've left me with no choice. On your knees, slave."

Her hackles lifted at the command and she glared at him until she faced facts. What did she think she was going to accomplish without a stitch on and no way of leaving the room? Maybe more to the point, he could starve her.

Hating herself and him, she sank to her knees on the hard floor.

"That's a piss-poor start. Head down with your ass in the air."

No way! She was a human being, not some whipped dog.

"You're going to regret this."

As he walked over to the dresser, she fought the impulse to beg him to forgive her, but pride kept her head up. He deposited the bag and water on the top of the dresser, opened a drawer and selected something. The sight of another leather strap like the one he'd used last night dried her throat and she started to lower her head.

He slapped the leather against his thigh. "Too late. Get up."

Confused, she hurried to her feet. Placing her hands over her crotch did nothing to hide herself from him, but she couldn't stop herself.

His mouth twitched and the sober look had returned. "Hands out with the insides of your wrists together."

She started shaking as she complied. As he tightened the strap around her wrists and fastened it so her inner wrists touched, she reminded herself that he'd given her the most mind-shattering climax of her life. For several minutes afterward she'd been unaware of the nipple clamps and had barely noticed the rush of circulation when he'd taken them off. He was capable of kindness. He had no intention of damaging her.

Didn't he?

"I haven't yet spelled out what constitutes acceptable behavior on your part," he said after letting her arms drop, "but that was on purpose because it's my responsibility to see if you'd learned anything from our first session."

"I did, Master." Her throat snagged at the last word. "You taught me a great deal."

"You aren't acting like it." He crouched and unlocked the chain from the bed. "You need to be a quick study." He straightened, grabbed her forced-together hands and pulled her to the middle of the room. "Maybe because I let you get off you think I'm going to cater to you, but you couldn't be more wrong."

"Master, I understand."

When he looked up, she did the same. A chain with a hook at the end hung from the ceiling directly above her. She'd already noted the ring imbedded in the strap. It wouldn't take any effort on his part to slide the hook through the ring.

"Master, I'm sorry. I didn't mean to displease you. That wasn't—"

"Unfortunately, it's too late. Lift your arms."

Please don't make me do this. A stern glare from him reinforced what she already knew. Begging for forgiveness wouldn't get her out of this mess. As, shaking again, she did as he'd commanded, her gaze fixed on the out-of-reach water bottle. Thirst seized her and it was all she could do not to beg.

Once she was on her toes with her arms stretched overhead, he grabbed them and lifted her off her feet. He hung her from the chain and let go. She dropped just enough that her toes scraped the floor.

"Master, Master, what are—"

"No questions. If you want sympathy from me you'd better stop whining."

The strain in her arms made her sick to her stomach. He stepped behind her and pushed. Knocked off her feet, she swung out only to swing back toward him. He held her against him with his breath on the back of her neck, then made her swing again.

"Not a word out of you, understand?" He sounded as if he'd memorized the words. "I'm not angry, but neither am I satisfied with your behavior. If you have any hope of pleasing me, you need to take your punishment."

This wasn't happening. No way could she be here, swaying back and forth with her toes dragging and Master's hands against her back keeping her going. She was losing feeling in her wrists.

Fortunately, before long, he left her and turned a lever

on the nearest wall. The chain started creaking. She was terrified he intended to hang her even higher. Instead, she settled onto the balls of her feet.

He returned to her and stroked her back. "What do you say?"

"Thank you, Master." The words rasped in her throat.

Head cocked, he looked at her. "Say it again."

Caught between gratitude and the desire to bury her nails in his flesh, she repeated herself.

"Good," he said and headed for the dresser again.

She came close to crying when he returned with the water bottle, and after he'd he removed the lid and held it to her mouth, she swallowed as fast as she could. Master controlled everything about her world.

"Master, thank you," she muttered.

"You're welcome," he whispered. "I wish I could believe you understand the meaning of the word 'master'."

Something about his tone caught her attention, but because he was already returning to the dresser she couldn't see his expression. The room was full of traps and she was a mouse with no way out. Anything she said or did might be wrong. She wouldn't know until it was too late.

As Master returned to her with a sandwich he'd taken out of the bag, fresh proof of his power slammed into her. She hated having her arms over her head but at least she could feel her fingers again and stand flat-footed. If that was what he wanted, she had no choice but to stay like this indefinitely. As unsettling as the possibility was, it paled next to knowing she couldn't do something as basic as feed herself.

"Let me guess." He tore off a piece and held it a few inches from her face so she had to lean toward the first food she'd had in more than twenty-four hours. "Right now you want me dead. If you could, you'd take great pleasure in doing it yourself."

The thought of him bleeding to death made her shudder. He hadn't given her permission to speak. Besides, all she cared about was the taste of peanut butter and jelly.

He waved another piece out of reach. "How would you do it? You grabbed a knife so I'm guessing knives are your weapons of choice. That was a mistake." He tapped his chest. "Maybe you're fantasizing about putting a bullet there." He touched the middle of his forehead. "Or here. Blow out my brains."

"No." She gasped. "I'd never—"

He held up his hand. "I don't want you lying to me."

"I'm not." She meant it. "All life has value."

He frowned and placed a piece in her mouth. "Even mine?"

Yes, she nearly told him, but it was too complicated. She chewed and swallowed. "My mother died shortly before I turned three. I have no memory of her. It shouldn't be like that for anyone."

She'd again forgotten to call him master, but judging by his expression, that wasn't what he was thinking about. If a private detective had been looking into her life, surely Tray knew her father had raised her. Maybe he hadn't considered that information important enough to hang on to.

Did he have a family? Maybe a wife and children somewhere?

No, she told herself as she waited for another bite. This man wouldn't be here if he was a father. Having children changed people, her father had told her. Babies taught adults the reward of selflessness.

The longer Tray remained silent, the less sure she was of what he was thinking. She'd be crazy to think he cared about her except in a master-slave way. Just because she couldn't imagine killing him didn't mean she wanted anything to do with him—not that she had a choice.

He finished feeding her in silence then ran his hands all over her, starting with her forearms and ending at her knees. He paid as much attention to her back as he did to her breasts and didn't make her spread her legs. Maybe he was checking her for injuries, but maybe he intended to keep her off-balance.

His touch did things to her she didn't understand. Of course she wanted to be left alone, to have back ownership of her body. At the same time the enforced intimacy reached her lonely heart. Losing her only parent so young had thrust her into the adult world before she'd been ready. Maybe she could have presented herself to the authorities and gone into foster care, but Dad had been a self-employed ranch hand and she'd been determined to honor his memory. When the couple Dad had been working for had offered her a job, she'd jumped at it. She'd slept in a room in the barn, shared meals with her employers and driven herself to school in Dad's pickup years before she had a driver's license. She'd had a few friends and several boyfriends, none of whom had known about her living situation. It hadn't taken long for her to accept that she was a loner. If that meant spending her life without a partner, so be it. Once she was settled financially she'd find a sperm donor and become a single parent.

Now, against her will, a man had taken over everything.

"You need cleaning up," he announced. He ran his fingers into her pubic hair. "And this gone."

She tried to look down at herself, but her breasts were in the way. Wondering how he intended to accomplish that tore her from unimportant thoughts, and she again stared at the man who'd claimed her.

"Shaved pussies are standard operating procedure around here," he continued. "Owners insist on being able to see the goods."

Again she berated herself for letting her mind get between her and survival. She'd ignored the all-knowing cameras while Master had fed her but as he unhooked her, she wondered who was watching and what those people thought of what was happening. The nudity that made her feel so vulnerable meant nothing to them. She was simply flesh, a marketable product. Not human.

Chapter Eleven

Tray lifted his trainee onto a high bathroom counter and reached for the straps below it. He hadn't removed her wrist restraints, but she tried to cover her pubic area. He spread her legs as wide as they'd go and closed the restraints around her ankles. If he'd wanted, he could have anchored her arms, but it wasn't as if she was going anywhere.

The setup complete, he stepped back and studied what he'd accomplished. She had that wide-eyed look, and he wondered if she was berating herself for not trying to run when she'd had the chance, except she'd never had one.

He'd read about her mother dying of cancer when she was little, but hadn't given that much thought. Instead, he'd fixed on her father's death in a farming accident. Along with realizing that the loss of her parents made her the kind of outsider Carnal was interested in, he'd wondered whether she'd had to finish growing up on her own. He hadn't expected to hear how much she valued life. Damn it, if he was going to concentrate on what he needed and wanted to accomplish, he had to stop thinking about what went on inside her head.

He reached into a drawer and pulled out a pair of scissors he could barely get his oversized fingers through. Trying to ignore how the metal pinched him, he grabbed hold of some of her pubic hair and cut it, careful not to touch her flesh.

Her bound hands hovered near his head while her legs jumped. He severed another hunk and placed the hairs on her thigh. Her pussy was so close, the smell of her earlier excitement invading his senses.

"This is a first?" he asked, not because he gave a damn whether she'd ever shaved herself there, but because he needed something beyond her sex to think about. "You've never done this before?"

"No." Her voice sounded strangled and her legs trembled even more. "Please don't..."

Ignoring the unfinished plea, he continued trimming her bush as short as he dared. He'd been given the opportunity to shave a couple of slaves, but not only had he removed just a bit of stubble, those females had been used to the operation. Sensing his slave's nervousness turned him on.

"This is a test," he said as she extended her fingers, stopping just short of touching his face. He wondered what that would feel like. "Lay a hand on me and you're going to regret it."

Her breath hissed and she leaned back, only to rock forward and stare down at her crotch as the blades neared her labia.

"You're scared, right?"

"Of course I am, Master."

Even though he resented her sharp retort, he had to give her points both for honesty and for remembering what to call him. He'd already done all the damage he could with the scissors, yet kept snipping at stray hairs. She'd tucked her useless hands under her chin and against her throat. Only once did she try to shift position on the counter, but he'd tied her so tightly she couldn't move. Trapping her nipples under metal earlier had awakened his sense of power, but this touched something even deeper. Before long she would be crouched before him with her head on the floor and her ass high for the taking. He'd partaken of a number of such offerings here so knew how damn good it felt. In contrast, altering her appearance took him somewhere he'd never been. He wasn't sure how he felt about what he was doing, almost as if he should apologize.

Hell no!

"This takes nudity to a new level," he said unnecessarily.

He worked his fingers out of the scissors' openings, put them back in the drawer and selected a razor. After putting it on the counter where she could see but not touch it, he started water running in the nearby sink. As he waited for the water to warm, he removed the lid from a can of shaving cream. Maybe the time would come when he'd tell her that his football injuries had forced him to comprehend helplessness, but maybe not. He dampened a washcloth and placed it over where her bush had been. That was when he realized he could expose her pussy even more. Whoever had modified this bathroom had planned for every possibility, as witnessed by the chain and hook hanging over and behind her.

He lifted her arms and stretched her out and back so her weight rested on her tailbone. After running the hook through the handy ring in the leather around her wrists, he activated a lever that stretched her even more. The way he'd positioned her, she could no longer see her pussy.

Time to see how she handled even more loss of self.

"What say we get this over with? I don't want you getting bored."

"I can't stop shaking. Don't cut me."

"What was that? An order? You should know better."

"That's not what I —"

He whipped off the washcloth and slapped her pussy. "This defiance of yours is getting tiresome. I can and *will* correct you as long and often as need be."

When she didn't respond, he took hold of her hair and bent her head forward so he had a clear view of her expression. She was overwhelmed but not defeated.

She returned his gaze. "I'm sorry, Master."

She wasn't, but if he took the time to try to change that, who knew when he'd finish getting her presentable according to Carnal standards? Management might even criticize his performance. Much as it galled him to admit it, he was still conditioned by years of doing what coaches expected.

"We'll talk about this later." He let go of her hair and pumped shaving cream into his hand, which he transferred to her mons. He hoped the camera captured her expression. He'd get there in terms of slave training, he just needed time.

Shaving the still-trembling slave took all his concentration, and undoubtedly longer than it did experienced trainers, but at last he was done. He again dampened the washcloth and wiped off the residual foam, going slowly so he could explore every inch of her sex. Whenever his mother had shaved her legs, she'd finished by applying hand cream, but that could wait here until his slave had taken another shower.

His slave. Not just a product he'd offer for sale when he was finished with her.

"How does this feel?" he asked, determined to silence the crazy thought. He lightly raked his fingers over her newly exposed flesh.

"Strange."

"That's all? Surely you can give me a better explanation. What about when I do this?" He rubbed her labia.

Her breath snagged. "I don't— What do you want me to say, Master?"

She might not have known it, but she'd stepped into a trap he intended to take advantage of. After planting his hands near the insides of her thighs, he caught her labia between thumbs and forefingers and drew them away from her body much as he'd done to her breasts earlier. She held her breath.

"I want a blow by blow of everything you're experiencing and make the explanation loud enough for your audience to hear."

She twisted her body marginally to the left then reversed direction. As he kept the tension going, he guessed she was trying to physically separate herself from what he was doing, which was the last thing he wanted. The two of them were going to get close, maybe dangerously so.

"Let me help you get started," he finally thought to say. "What part of your body are you most aware of?"

"My pussy."

"What about it?"

A long, shuddering breath had him thinking she was debating saying anything. Unfortunately, when a master issued a command, a slave obeyed. He increased the tension.

Her leg muscles tightened. "You—you have hold of it. It feels as if it no longer belongs to me."

Because he hadn't expected that much honesty, he backed off until she stopped trying to lift herself off the counter. When he drew her sex lips apart, moisture glistened in the dark hole. He could lose himself in it, forget how to talk if he wasn't careful.

"You want back ownership of your sex, right?" he asked. "Maybe you're praying you can trust me to be careful."

She struggled to sit upright. "I want..."

"No, no, partial responses aren't acceptable. Give it another try."

Her head fell back and she relaxed, which made him wonder if she'd given up. Thinking that was what it might be reminded him who held the power so he released her lips and cupped his hand over her sex. He pressed, wiggling his fingers as he did.

"Oh!"

"Oh what?"

"I'm, ah, afraid of you," she muttered through clenched teeth. "I don't want to be, but I can't help it."

I don't want you to be. "That's better, more honest. Go on."

Her breasts rose and fell as she breathed. She'd nearly stopped shaking, but he wasn't deluded enough to think she might already be with the program.

"This won't end until I tell you what you want to hear," she muttered. "I understand."

What would it take to extinguish her fire—if he really wanted to? "Just say it then."

"Master, nothing like this has ever happened to me. I, ah, I know a woman who was raped but I never was. I never…"

Not that it mattered, considering what he was doing to her, but he was glad to hear that. He'd always considered rapists to be animals. Still embracing her pussy, he started moving his hand back and forth, maybe massaging her.

"Ah," she whispered.

"Ah what?"

She didn't respond, but he kept going. Her useless movements continued and her breathing became labored.

"Sucks to be a member of the female sex, doesn't it?" he teased and slipped a forefinger into her opening. "Especially one with a healthy sexual appetite. Are you still afraid of me?"

"Yes," she said after a pause. Her head remained against the wall behind her, her eyes now hooded.

He worked his finger deeper. "Because you're scared I'm going to hurt you?"

"Yes."

Damn it, why had he asked that question and was there really a distinction between rape and what he was doing? He needed there to be one. "What else?"

She jolted only to fall back again. "I don't— I don't want you to know—"

"It's my right." Determined to live in the moment without too much thinking, he started pumping. "I can't consider my job complete until you have no secrets left." That was what Robert and the others had told him. "Maybe you're hung up wondering when I'm going to put a butt plug in your rear opening."

Once again she tried to sit upright, which she couldn't do because her arms were so far behind her. "Please don't, Master."

She sounded less self-contained and more unsure. Now he was getting somewhere, living up to Carnal expectations. "I'm not going to start prepping you for back door action today. Back to the issue at hand." He worked a second finger next to the one already inside her and began a thrusting action. Her juices flooded his fingers.

Come to me. Become what you were meant to be.

"What, beside fear, are you experiencing?"

She'd almost stopped rocking her head, but the movement picked up. At the same time, shudders moved wavelike throughout her.

"Arousal. I don't want to be like this, but I can't stop myself."

"I don't blame you." Why hadn't he thought to bring in the vibrator? In the wake of what he'd put her through earlier, it shouldn't take much to push her off the edge. "It isn't as if you have anything else to think about, and you can't do anything except sit there with your legs apart."

The hand he'd placed against her pussy was at an awkward angle. Vowing to get to her before he had to quit, he ran his free hand under her buttocks and worked his middle finger between her ass cheeks. He continued fucking her channel.

"Still aroused? Maybe I'm boring you."

"No, oh no." Her toes curled and her fingers clenched. Goosebumps appeared on her sides. Once, twice, her inner muscles tightened around his fingers. Then she must have found a measure of self-control because she stopped fucking him back. "Trying—trying so hard not to— I don't want— You can't make me..."

"Ah, but I can. I already have." He felt strong, good, no longer conflicted. "Why the hell don't you want to come?"

The muscles on the sides of her neck stood out and hard as she was clenching her teeth, he hoped she didn't break one. He admired her determination. At the same time, his own resolve grew. He didn't need a vibrator to get to her, and the sooner she understood that, the better.

He kept his nails short. Just the same, he didn't want to take a chance on injuring her bung hole, so he settled for finger-plugging it. Obviously it had made an impact, because she kept trying to levitate. She might have stood a better chance of pulling it off if he stopped fucking her sex hole, but he didn't.

"Here we go again," he teased. "Too bad you're still at a disadvantage. Like it or not, I'm going to win this round."

"Not fair! Damn it, not fair."

Instead of ramming her outburst down her throat as he was expected to do, he shrugged. "Life isn't fair. Some days are worse than others. Guess which today is."

Her mouth opened then closed, leaving him to wonder what she'd stopped herself from saying.

It took some doing, but he managed to contort his upper body enough to latch onto a breast with his mouth. He could have held on if he used his teeth, which he wasn't about to do. However, judging by her ragged sobs, he'd accomplished what he'd set out to do.

She was trapped and knew it, was helpless to stop him from assaulting her. He nibbled on her other breast, holding on longer than he had with the first one and applying a little more pressure.

"Master, oh, Master."

Her whimper ended his moments of self-recrimination. He started to turn from her so he could stare at the mirror when it dawned on him that maybe she was winning this round after all. Now that she was aroused, all she needed was to climax to feel good about how the time in the bathroom had gone. A little more effort on his part and she'd be gone.

"That's enough," he announced and jerked back his hands. He held them up so she could see that the right one was slick with her juices. "You haven't earned this."

Chapter Twelve

During her first few months as a paid jockey, Marina had come home every day feeling as if she'd been beaten up. Even a hot shower and aspirin hadn't completely eased her aching muscles. Then she'd started lifting weights on a regular basis. As a result, unless she was thrown, she no longer hurt after a long day at the race track.

In undeniable contrast, Master's methods had left her feeling as if he'd been pounding on her. She might not have had bruises and he hadn't broken her flesh, but she couldn't remember ever feeling this sensitive.

After denying her a climax, he'd unfastened her legs and arms and let her step into the shower. This time he hadn't joined her, but even with the steam, he'd undoubtedly seen every inch of her as she'd soaped and rinsed. He'd ordered her to get out and stand before him, then had thoroughly dried her. The feel of terrycloth against her newly denuded pussy was both unnerving and sensual. When he was done, he'd produced some cream and slathered it all over her. If that wasn't enough intimacy, he'd ordered her to spread her legs and used a different cream around her sex organs. Within seconds the abraded sensation there ended. A little later she'd started to feel overly warm between her legs.

"A special Carnal treatment," he'd told her as he'd fastened her hands behind her and again tethered her to the bed.

Hours had passed before she'd stopped feeling hot and aroused down there. If she'd had use of her hands she would have masturbated to what would have been an easy climax, but he'd made sure she couldn't. He'd left her alone most of the time, and although she'd wanted to lie down, having her hands behind her stopped her. As a result, she'd had no choice but to sit on the side of the bed waiting for Master to return.

Finally, he had. He'd fed her another sandwich and held two bottles of water for her to drink. After helping her use the toilet, he'd again harnessed her to the damn bed. He'd left without saying a word.

His silence was harder on her nerves than not being able to do anything. After she'd eaten, she'd tried to ask him what he intended to do with her, but had stopped when he'd slapped her breasts. The message had stuck. He'd tell her what he wanted her to know when it entertained him to do so. She had no choice but to wait.

At least he'd returned after dark, and again had silently taken her into the bathroom. Afterward, he'd anchored her to the bed with a collar and chain. As she'd tried to fall asleep under the blanket he'd thrown over her, she'd told herself to be grateful because at least she had back use of her arms and legs. She could have masturbated, but by then the cream had worn off and she couldn't bring herself to touch that part of her body. She hated thinking about how helpless she'd been while he'd shaved her where she'd never felt a razor.

* * * *

Morning had found its way through the small, high window by the time Master opened the door and entered. She didn't know how long she'd been awake, long enough for her bladder to feel full, and dread that he'd abandoned her to have seeped into her pores. Her heartbeat kicked up at the sight of him, but she told herself it was only because he'd become the provider of food, water and bathroom breaks.

"Lesson three coming up." He threw a piece of dry toast on the bed, followed by a small bottle she guessed held orange juice. "Time to get you ready."

Even though he hadn't given her permission to eat, she started chewing on the toast. At least it had grains in it and provided some sustenance. The orange juice was cold and tasted wonderful. When she was done, she placed her hands in her lap. Her fingers glided over her exposed mons.

He unfastened the neck chain from the bed but didn't take off the collar. As she walked ahead of him into the bathroom, the chain rubbed between her breasts and legs, prompting her to hold it out from her body. She'd checked earlier so knew she couldn't remove the leather collar. At least whoever had made it had placed something soft, fur maybe, next to her flesh.

After she'd used the toilet, he handed her a toothbrush.

"Thank you, Master," she said.

He responded with a grunt. After she'd brushed her teeth, he lifted her back onto the counter. Anticipation had her shaking again. He took hold of her nipples, prompting her to clench her fists to keep from trying to push him away.

"Yesterday we had a discussion about my expectation that you always be honest with me. I trust you remember it."

Nodding, she stared at his hands.

"You made a halfway decent start but need a lot of improvement." His hold tightened, causing shockwaves to race through her breasts. "What are you thinking right now?"

Just say it. You know what he wants. "That I don't want this to be happening."

"By *this* do you mean having your nipples pinched or would you prefer you'd never seen me?"

That would be wonderful. She'd have her life back. But if she'd never met him, she wouldn't know what it really meant to be alive.

"My nipples hurt, Master. I want that to stop."

"Of course you do. I'm going to offer you a trade. I'll release your boobs and you'll shove more cream up your pussy."

It wasn't really an offer, because this big man would do what he wanted.

"Repeat after me," he said after a moment. "I'll fill my pussy with cream, Master, because that's what you want, and if it pleases you to drill holes through my nipples and fill them with gold rings, I'll stand there and let you do it."

Just like that she turned cold. She couldn't stop herself from gripping his wrists and trying to pull his hands off her.

"I can't. I won't!"

He shook his head. "I shouldn't have to tell you this. You don't have permission to touch me. That's a hard and fast Carnal rule. I'm going to have to punish you."

For what, acting instinctively? Feeling trapped, she let go of his wrists. He squeezed her nipples, sending more fire through them. Then he released them. Relief lasted only until he took the pussy lubricant out of a cabinet.

"Do it." He handed the tube to her.

She was more agile than him and maybe faster. If there was such a thing as fair between them, she might be able to get away, but he wouldn't let that happen. At least he wasn't punishing her. She'd take what pleasure she could. Careful not to look at him or the relentless camera, she unscrewed the lid and squeezed a dollop onto her fingers. Her fingers warmed as she leaned back. She had to place the chain over her shoulder to get to her pussy. Contributing to her *abuse* was demeaning but she had no choice.

At first the sensation was pleasant, then it became sensual coupled with hot. By the time she'd placed three dollops inside herself, she was turned on. She squeezed her thighs together, only to be distracted when he yanked her off the counter via the chain. As he hauled her back into the bedroom, she heard a soft female cry and knew it came from the room on the other side of the bathroom. What was happening to the woman she'd seen yesterday?

Master grabbed her by the shoulders and forced her

backward into a corner. "You do *not* ever touch me unless I've given you permission, understand? There are consequences for both of us."

"I understand, Master."

"Too late." He stared down at her until she felt like a bug about to be squashed. "I have no choice but to punish you."

Am I going to enjoy it?

Chapter Thirteen

All too soon, Marina stood under the chain that had kept her arms over her head yesterday. This time her arms were behind her, with straps around her wrists and elbows so her elbows nearly touched. She'd stupidly resisted being trussed up, but of course it hadn't done any good. Master had secured the overhead chain to her wrists and drawn the chain upward, forcing her to lean over. Her breasts dangled and her hair kept getting in her eyes. The chain attached to her collar—how she hated thinking of the collar as *hers*—dangled to the floor. Maybe she should have reconciled herself to severe restraints, but she wasn't. A single thought kept running through her—Master could do anything he wanted to her. Her tingling pussy wasn't enough of a distraction.

"I shouldn't have to spell everything out to you." He waved a gag in front of her. This one resembled a bridle with a wooden bit and straps designed to go around and over her head. "You should have known you have no right to lay a hand on me."

Nothing she said would change what was about to happen so she decided to fight in the only way she could. She wasn't a whipped dog. No matter what happened, she refused to demean herself—somehow. Besides, she'd sensed something, humanity maybe, in him. "Your hands have been all over me. That's what isn't fair."

He clamped his hand around her neck. Even with the collar there, he cut off her ability to breathe.

"Listen to me, slave. You *will* learn to obey. You have no choice. It doesn't matter to me how long it takes" He paused. "In fact, your resistance turns me on." He looked down at his crotch. "Something for you to think about."

The only thing she could put her mind to was getting oxygen into her lungs. As fear continued its inroad, she tried to back away, but the effort threatened to pull her shoulders out of their sockets. Defeated, she stopped resisting. Her sex remained hot, eager, the one good thing.

She was lightheaded by the time he released her neck. He let her draw in a few breaths then forced the wooden bit against her teeth. When she opened her mouth, he shoved the bit in and fastened it. He patted her cheek.

"The cry you heard a few minutes ago was the sound of another master educating his slave. I could allow you to express yourself in the same way, but I hate the sound of screaming. This way I can focus on making my lesson stick and not have to listen to you howl."

Why did he say words like howl? They only made her feel lost. She tried to reach him human to human, but he placed his hand over her eyes, blinding her.

"I'm not stupid. I know what you're trying. It isn't going to work."

She was somewhat relieved when he allowed her to see again. However, waiting for him to begin whatever he intended to do to her gave her too much time to think. Was this the lesson he'd planned for today, or had her touching his wrists changed everything?

"You're property," he told her. "Still human and yet not. You no longer have any rights. Your owner can use you any way he sees fit. He can pass you around to his friends, buy favors with your body, keep you silent for the rest of your life. Maybe you'll never see sunlight again."

The last statement unhinged her more than the others had. For the first time since her capture, tears burned her eyes. His hands at his sides, he stared at her. She thought he might demand an explanation, which would necessitate removing the gag, but even though she sensed his confusion, he didn't speak. Instead he wiped away a tear and deposited it on her breast.

A sound distracted her. Looking up, she realized the man and woman who'd come into the bathroom yesterday had joined them. The man, who was balding and not particularly tall, wore jeans and no shirt. He was muscular, but nothing like her master. The woman — Marina refused to call her a slave — was still naked. Her legs were held apart via a spreader bar attached to her ankles. As a result, she waddled more than walked. Her hands were restrained under her chin as Master had done to her. She wasn't gagged.

"Thought we'd watch," the other man said. "Where's her butt plug? I thought you were going to fit her with one this morning."

"Change of plans," Master said and went on to describe her *crime* to his fellow trainer.

"She broke rule number one. You have no choice but to punish her. Nip resistance in the bud. Mind if I park this one somewhere and watch your technique?"

Master frowned. "I realize I'm new at this, but I don't appreciate being critiqued."

The man shrugged and rested a hand on the woman's flank. "I've only been at this a year, so I remember what it was like having someone looking over my shoulder. Believe me, I'll keep my mouth shut. The way I see it, there's more than one way of getting things done."

Although Master still didn't look convinced, he nodded. "How are things coming with your subject?"

The man cupped the woman's hairless mons. "She's getting there. Up until a week ago she occasionally fought me, but the conditioning I've been giving her has made an impact."

Marina didn't want to think about what he meant by 'conditioning'. Just seeing the woman's lack of expression was enough. Would that be her before long? She'd stop caring what happened to her?

Master returned to the dresser and selected a riding crop

and short leash with a clip on either end. Even though the crop wasn't as sturdy as the one she'd rarely used during races, it alarmed her. Master put it down and stepped behind her. Not being able to see him added to her fear, and she thought back to when she'd gone to see several mustangs that had been rounded up so they could be sold and trained. She'd debated buying one, but had been outbid. Some of the wild horses had been so scared she'd longed to go into the corral and reassure them.

A pulling sensation at the back of her head told her Master had clipped the leash to the gag and was using it to lift her head. He attached the leash to something behind her, leaving her body arched and looking into the eyes of the woman standing opposite her. Sympathy flickered through the other prisoner.

Thank you, Marina tried to tell her. *This way I don't feel so alone, and I know you're alive.*

Master retrieved the crop and held it close to her face. "I have no doubt you know what this is and what it's used for. In fact, I selected it with your former career in mind. You wielded it to encourage more speed out of a horse. My goal is to encourage obedience from you. It'll make it easier in the long run."

Was everyone associated with this operation called Carnal crazy? How dare they think they could do these things to another human being? She stamped her foot because it was the only thing she could do. Sensation sparked in her pussy, distracting her anew.

"Lots of defiance in her," the man said. "When I started out I thought the most important thing was to extinguish rebellion. That was before I realized how much fun playing with spirit is." He again grabbed his captive's mons, shaking it this time. "Beats putting up with one who's more dead than alive."

The other woman wasn't dying, just dispirited. Marina vowed to never let that happen to her. She no longer thought in terms of life plans. Now everything revolved around getting through one day at a time.

"That's what I'm most concerned about." Master slapped his palm with the crop. The faint thud started her shivering. "I need to focus on finding and keeping that middle ground."

"Some buyers don't care whether there's any sparks left."

Master slapped his palm again. "That's sick."

Not just that, she wanted to scream. Everything Carnal existed for was demented.

Master positioned himself in front of her and so close she felt his breath on her scalp. "Your body belongs to me. There's no equality here and never will be." He tapped her cheek with the crop. She tried to swing away but couldn't. "It's probably wasted effort telling you to think of my body as a temple, but by the time we finish today, I hope you'll never impulsively touch another man. You certainly won't try to stop him from doing what he wants with you. If you don't get it—" He briefly closed his eyes. "There's always tomorrow for another lesson."

She got it. Subservience was expected and enforced here. If he let her speak, she'd give him the apology he wanted. He didn't need to string her up, and he certainly didn't need to use that *thing* on her.

"You're naked," he said unnecessarily. "You'll remain naked as long as I see fit." He cocked his arm and connected with her right breast. The crop stung, but she could handle it. She'd survive.

And maybe gain his respect.

"I know what you're thinking," he continued. "That you've heard that before, so why am I boring you by repeating what you already know." He slapped her other breast, a little harder this time. "Because the message that's my responsibility to give hasn't yet been drummed into you." Another blow, this one landing on her right breast again. "For one thing, you remember having clothes. You keep thinking you'll return to that state."

He started slapping her breasts in earnest. Even though

she was pretty sure the crop wouldn't break her skin and didn't cause that much pain, the nonstop quality of her beating reinforced her helplessness. Master had all but immobilized her. There was nowhere she could go. He could, and might, keep this up for hours.

She hissed into the bit the instant he shifted to her thighs. Now that he was no longer focusing on her breasts, he was putting more strength behind the blows. Desperate to do something, anything, to distract herself, she started lifting and lowering her legs like a horse excited for a race to begin. This wasn't a race though. She'd already forgotten the start and had no idea when it would end, if it did. Her thighs burned. There was no way she could stop dancing in place — dancing to his tune.

Feeling alive in ways she'd never imagined possible.

He started moving to her right. She forced herself in the same direction a few inches. "Whoa up," the other man said. "I don't think you want her doing that."

"You're right."

While running the crop down her side, Master grabbed the chain hanging from her collar. He drew the chain out and crouched. A clicking sound had her trying to see what he'd done but she was locked in place. He'd harnessed her to something on the floor, completely immobilizing her head.

Not one day at a time but a single moment. Surviving heartbeat by heartbeat.

"That's more like it." Master tapped the crop against her cheeks. "You look lovely."

Lovely? Even though she couldn't see herself, she wouldn't be surprised if she couldn't recognize herself. Undoubtedly the cameras remained trained on her. Maybe whoever had told Carnal about her was watching. Laughing. High-fiving.

Caught. In ways she'd never believed possible.

Desired.

Shocked by the thought, she struggled to examine it. Self-assured men somewhere wanted her.

106

"Back to work," Master said. "Hopefully you haven't forgotten what this is about."

How can I, she longed to throw at him. He was teaching her a lesson, training her, separating her from self-confidence and independence.

Giving her life new meaning.

She didn't have time to consider where that thought had come from because Master started striking her again. He repeatedly slapped her left thigh which was already on fire. After maybe a half dozen blows, he moved so she could barely glimpse him out of the corner of her eye. The crop started landing on the outside of her thigh, the blows random.

"Submit," he muttered. "Submit. If you remember nothing else, remember that."

Her arms ached. The bit made her feel less than human, and she could barely twitch, let alone move. Master kept after her, *swat, swat, swat* until she could no longer distinguish between where she hurt and where she didn't. Like the other time she'd been gagged, she was drooling.

He was behind her now, spanking her with what had been a tool of her trade. Occasionally he stroked the small of her back, and she relaxed when he did. The gentle touches never lasted. Every time the blows started up, she felt as if she was starting over, simply trying to survive.

The other man had pulled his captive around so Marina had no choice but to stare at her. As Master subjected her to his definition of punishment, she saw what she knew was her expression mirrored in the silent woman's eyes. The naked stranger no longer looked dull and drugged. She kept wincing. She also occasionally stared at Marina's wildly jerking breasts. Was the other woman turned on?

It seemed impossible, and yet there was something erotic about facing a woman who couldn't close her legs, one whose glistening labia were on display. Studying denuded female sex distracted Marina from her punishment.

Life at its most basic.

"Dirty little cunt," Master said softly as he worked his way around her right side. "What a sweaty, dirty bitch you are. Who's going to want you the way you are now? You have no value. You're dirt, a reject."

She wasn't! Wealthy, dominant men wanted her.

The crop repeatedly landed on her flank, just missing her hip bone. "Think about this. It's possible you'll be bought by some foreigner who'll ship you overseas. Maybe he'll park you in his harem. Maybe he'll keep you in a basement, only bring you out when he owes someone a favor."

Marina realized Master was messing with her mind. The awful thing was it was working. She had no voice, no clothes and no way of protecting herself. Maybe Master intended to keep her in a collar. He might punish her every day, might restrain her at different times and in different ways so she'd never know what to expect when. Maybe he'd feed her nothing but dry toast, not let her shower, wipe her ass because she couldn't do it herself.

She guessed Master intended to strike her right side at least as many times as he had her left and that had been what, hundreds? No, not that many, but more than she could handle.

On fire. Frighteningly sensitive in so many places. Drool dropping onto her breasts, and she was still doing that damnable unproductive dance.

I'll wait him out, she told herself during a moment of clarity. He was nearly back to where he'd started and must be nearly done. He no longer threw demeaning words at her. Maybe he'd said all he intended to and considered the lesson well-delivered.

Then what?

What if he was just getting started?

Something landed on the floor near her. Master held up the hand that had been wielding the crop so she could see he no longer had it. If she could've spoken, she would have thanked him. He unhooked the leash attached to the back of her gag, then released the chain in front so she could move her head. Having back this small bit of freedom lifted her spirits. Her body was no longer under attack. Maybe that was why she noticed that moisture was tracking down the insides of the other woman's legs.

"That's it?" the newcomer asked. "You're done?"

"With the first part, yes." Master patted her cheek.

"Got it." The other man grabbed his captive's nipples and jerked down, forcing her awkwardly onto her knees. "Watching you work your slave over has gotten me hot and bothered. Time for a little stress relief."

From what Marina could tell, there'd been little communication between the other two, but the woman must have known what the man wanted because she lifted her cuffed hands and unzipped him. As a long, thick cock emerged, she leaned toward him and opened her mouth. He grabbed her hair with both hands so he could anchor her while thrusting into her.

Slurping sounds, coupled with the man's now-rapid breathing, gave Marina something other than her stinging body to concentrate on. She'd twice happened upon couples having sex. Both times she'd left as fast as possible. Now there was no not seeing a woman suck on the cock being repeatedly driven into her mouth. The woman made no effort to get away. In fact, judging by how her buttocks kept clenching, she wanted this almost as much as the man did.

"Obviously," Master said, "modesty doesn't mean much here. Watching you being punished turned them both on. It doesn't look as if they give a damn what you and I do."

Was Master saying he expected the same from her? In the aftermath of the harsh demonstration of his domination over her, she knew better than to oppose him. What would his cock filling her mouth feel like? Maybe she'd gag as she'd done the few times she'd tried fellatio. Maybe he'd show her what he wanted from her and in the giving she'd please him.

Pleasing Master?

Was that something she wanted?

Before she could ask where the insane thought had come from, he unfastened the gag and drew it out of her mouth. Beyond grateful, she licked her lips.

"Thank you, Master." She straightened until the strain in her arms stopped her. "I'm grateful."

He grabbed her chin and forced her to look into his eyes. "Say that again."

"Thank you for your kindness, Master."

"Good. I wasn't sure I'd hear that so soon. Maybe it's time to see where your new attitude will take us."

He left her long enough to release the tension on the chain attached to the elbow restraint. Even though she was still tethered to the chain and couldn't use her arms, she felt so free she almost dismissed the remaining restraints. She looked at her legs. Her flesh where he'd struck her was reddened but she didn't see any bruising or blood.

"Thank you, Master," she repeated and wiggled her fingers so, hopefully, he knew what she was talking about.

"I'm not letting you stand upright out of the goodness of my heart." He tapped her cheek, startling her. "Taking pity on a slave is a foreign concept around here." He sighed. "I have no use for an injured slave."

Despite his hard words, she couldn't help but wonder if maybe he had had sympathy for her after all.

Was it possible he cared about her as a human being?

"You showed courage in taking your punishment." He began kneading her breasts, and even though the pressure reawakened her over-stimulated nerves there, causing discomfort, she stood her ground. He jerked his head at the cameras. "They're waiting for the next chapter. Let's see if you can give them their money's worth."

Imagining others getting off on her being punished made her wish she could climb into the camera and assault them. How could she have thought she wanted to enter their world? Master used his hold on her nipples to turn her so her back was to the other couple. It didn't matter that the camera she'd occasionally stared at while being beaten was behind her because there were others, all showing her naked body in full color. Who might be watching? The image of an opulent room filled with self-assured older men smoking cigars, drinking expensive whiskey and jerking off, came to mind.

Coming at her expense.

"I don't have to tell you this," he said, "but I'm going to because it'll give you something else to think about. Even before your capture, pictures of you were being sent to potential buyers. Now that you're a Carnal *guest* and your training has begun, certain Carnal staff are assessing the amount and kind of interest there is in you." He'd let go of her nipples once he had her in position, but now took back control of them. He moved them about as if checking their mobility, leaving her to deal with the sensation, coupled with her freshly beaten body and hot pussy. She'd never been treated like this. The only thing she knew for certain was that Master orchestrated everything.

"You may be pleased," he said, "to know you've garnered considerable interest. In fact, this morning a senior member of Carnal management told me he believes you're going to go for more than the majority of the product we put out."

You can't be serious! Damn it, human beings aren't for sale.

But not only wasn't that true, she was in no position to argue with Master—Master, who'd just beaten her and left her tied up. Master, who could control her simply by holding onto her nipples.

This massive man had stormed into her world and ripped her from it. He'd done things to her she'd never imagined anyone would ever do and yet she was standing before him, not protesting.

Feeling different.

Wondering what he intended to do next and how long it would be before he rammed his cock into her pussy.

How that would make her feel.

Chapter Fourteen

Tray had called himself a bastard more than once, but if he'd ever meant it more, he didn't remember. Repeatedly hitting his trainee—it was better if he didn't think of her by name—with the crop had been easier than he'd thought it would be but, in retrospect, that's what bothered him the most. Watching videos of slaves being punished for punishment's sake had been a surreal experience, almost like watching a movie and knowing what he was seeing wasn't actually happening. The first time he'd seen a Carnal video, he'd been appalled but hadn't said anything. Before long, however, he'd convinced himself that repeatedly being exposed to harsh training sessions would prepare him for actually doing it, but as he'd dug through the dresser for what he'd intended to use on her, he knew he'd been wrong. Bottom line, he felt like a monster because she hadn't stood a chance.

That wasn't all he'd felt.

The truth was, laying into her had turned him on. The whole time he'd been punishing her, he'd enjoyed seeing her sweating, straining body. So what if that made him a bastard in her eyes, it was the truth. He *was* a bastard. He wouldn't be here if he wasn't. He'd been tempted to keep going after her just to see her dance to his tune, but had stopped because Carnal brass expected him to take her to the next level. And she deserved it.

He'd loosened her bonds and given her back the ability to speak, but damned if he wished he hadn't started anything. She deserved to be on horseback, riding to win until she couldn't do that any longer. What goddamned right did he have to rob her of her life?

The right of might.

Still conflicted, he selected the tools he needed and returned to his subject. Subject, not a lovely and once-free young woman. After letting her see what he had, he placed the items on the floor near her feet. Cliff and his slave in training were still going at it, both so into what they were doing they probably didn't care what was happening around them. He'd been surprised by Cliff's slave's arousal. Could he take his slave to the same place?

He'd try. Get her trained. Watch her being auctioned off. Choose his next subject. Stop thoughts that threatened to keep him awake at night.

"I'm not going to waste time explaining what's about to happen," he told her. "Unless you're stupid, which you aren't, you'll get it." There was something about standing this close to her with her gaze locked on him that made him wish they were alone. It wasn't as if he wanted to connect with her, nothing like that, damn it, but despite what she'd been through, her bright eyes spoke of layers. She might be more complex than he was.

He unclipped the chain and removed the collar. She started to rotate her neck, but he grabbed her hair, stopping her.

"Don't get any ideas that things are going to change. I'm simply exchanging the generic Carnal model for one I had designed."

She blinked several times and her mouth tightened, which surprised him because she must have noticed the metal collar he'd placed on the floor. Maybe the other items had distracted her, maybe she was caught somewhere in those layers he'd sensed. He wasn't sure how he felt about that, more unbalanced than he wanted to admit. Wasn't she supposed to be a body, living flesh to mold and manipulate and enjoy?

When he'd initially sketched the inch-wide silver band with four equally-spaced rings imbedded in it, he'd looked forward to seeing it against a pale throat. He'd been particularly pleased with how his name etched in black had turned out, and the tiny electronic locking device. The Carnal craftsman had shown the finished product around, and since then, three other trainers had requested the same design.

Unlike the leather and wool affair she'd been wearing, this collar had no padding. The edges were rounded and it was loose enough not to constrict her breathing. A hinge allowed him to open it enough to place it around her neck and after clicking it closed, he could barely see the locking seam.

He hooked a finger through the ring in front and demonstrated how easily he could control her, not that she didn't already know. Robert and whoever else was monitoring his performance might not approve, but her elbows had been unnaturally close long enough so he took off the strap binding them and massaged her arms. Judging by her breathing, she was having trouble not moving. Robert had warned him that she might react like a wild animal and be willing to risk injuring herself trying to get free, but so far she'd mostly exhibited admirable self-control.

Releasing her elbows had also freed her from the overhead chain, so he clipped it to the back of her new collar. "I want to draw your attention to your latest adornment's versatility," he said. "I had it designed specifically for times like this. It's cumbersome to have to change things out all the time."

When she didn't respond, he reached down for the dildo and butt plug. Cliff started grunting before he could decide whether to give her a demonstration of their power. Against Tray's better judgment, he turned his attention to the *entertainment*. Cliff was rocking with his spine arched and his hands buried in his fuck-partner's hair. At what Tray figured was the last moment, Cliff shoved her away so his cock popped out of her mouth. Cum sprayed her face.

"No," his slave muttered.

He turned his attention to her, but by then she'd closed

her mouth. He tried to imagine doing the same thing. She was little more than a receptacle after all, a handy outlet for men's sexual energy—at least that's what he'd been told and had believed he'd bought in to. Why then, did subjecting her to something she must see as a degrading act feel wrong? It was one thing if she wanted cum dripping off her chin, quite another if she hated it.

Damn it, where are those thoughts coming from? "Turn around," he barked. "You've seen enough."

His subject took a second longer than necessary to obey, time enough for him to realize she feared not being able to see him. Her spine and rounded buttocks brought him back into the space he'd occupied while he'd been striking her. She was unmolded clay and he the artist charged with turning her into something beautiful.

"Legs apart," he commanded.

A second passed before she complied. He pushed against her shoulder blades with his forearm until her back was parallel to the floor, which caused the restraining chain attached to her collar to tighten. Otherwise, he would have forced her to bend even lower.

After picking it up, he opened the tube of lube and generously covered what he intended to plug her with, then swiped the rubber dildo over her slit. She tried to rise onto her toes but couldn't. Moisture coated the insides of her sex lips. Maybe the cream already in her was responsible, maybe she was remembering the climaxes he'd forced on her yesterday.

"Spread them." He tapped the insides of her thighs. "Put the goodies where I can get my hands on them."

She muttered something he didn't catch, but at least she complied, not that she had a choice. How many pussies had he seen and explored? More than he could remember, probably more than most men. He should be used to this part of a woman's body, and it should no longer automatically turn him on, but today it did. Her sex was open and available to him, a perpetual gift.

Except he'd promised he wouldn't rape her.

Chapter Fifteen

Despite knowing what Master intended to do, Marina couldn't help but shudder as he inserted one of the *things* into her vaginal opening. She'd wondered if it would hurt, but it slid right in. As she tried to acclimate herself to the invasion, she reluctantly admitted that being the recipient of Master's attention had turned her on. Instead of loathing him for having beaten-trained her, she needed this connection between them. He had something new in mind, something that hopefully wouldn't include a crop or whip.

Her thoughts shifted as he pushed the dildo deep. Large as it was, it would remain there as long as she was bent over. She'd shivered when the intrusion had begun. Now she waited for it to start moving. What did she care whether the other two saw what Master was doing to her? This was about her and the man who'd locked his collar around her neck.

Master was no longer holding the dildo in place. That meant—oh no—that meant he was getting ready to insert the butt plug. Her throat tightened and it took all her self-restraint to remain in position. She'd never so much as imagined what one felt like and now—now—

"Relax," he told her. "Breathe."

Despite the warning, the pressure against her back door startled her. She started to lift her head but a slap on her buttocks stopped her. The unnerving pressure eased then increased, separating tissues unaccustomed to the strain. This was only the beginning. Day by day, he'd subject her to larger plugs until she could accommodate a man's penis. She'd be considered valuable and versatile, an all-around sex slave capable of satisfying her master in every way. Maybe he'd put her on display or invite his friends to a party where she was the main entertainment.

Why couldn't she close down her imagination? And if not that, why couldn't she mentally take herself to where Master didn't exist?

The plug was taking over, tension continuing to grow, plowing deeper, pushing wider. Her legs shook and her breath whistled. Master kept guiding the plug into her, but that wasn't all. He started turning the dildo one way then the other so it randomly pressed against her vaginal walls. The only thing she truly knew was that her body was being taken over, filled, stuffed.

"Listen to me," he said. "You are listening, aren't you?"

I don't want to. "Yes."

He pushed on both so-called tools. "Yes who?"

"Master. Yes, I'm listening, Master."

"That's better. Marginally. One more thing for me to do and you can stand up. I'll even let you move around."

The notion of walking with her holes occupied nearly made her laugh when there was nothing funny about this. She waited because she had choice, because Master's domination was starting to feel, what, maybe right?

Trying to comprehend why she kept having these unwanted thoughts left her ill-prepared for the leather belt he was placing around her waist. A wide strap hung down in front.

"Straighten. Keep your legs apart."

She did as Master commanded but saw herself as if from a distance, felt things that were happening to someone else. Master wasn't guiding the strap between her legs and pulling it against her crotch. He wasn't fastening the strap to the belt in back, tightening the belt, or snugging the strap — but he was.

Disbelieving, she looked down at the leather band against her belly and disappearing between her legs. It wasn't painful, but it rested snugly over the dual insertions. Master had taken her to yet another level, had forced her to the edge of yet another physical and emotional journey.

"There." He planted his hands on her waist and turned her to face him.

Had he become taller in the short amount of time her back had been to him? Maybe his shoulders had widened. One thing she had no doubt of, his focus was on her.

And why wouldn't it be? There she was, his slave in training waiting for hell to begin. No, not hell. Something she couldn't, wouldn't give a name to.

"That's how you should be." He cupped her chin and lifted her head so they shared the same breath. "A sexual creature I created."

Her arms remained locked behind her, which maybe was why she couldn't concentrate on anything except what he'd brought to life between her legs. Even though she suspected he'd disapprove, she tried to close her legs, only to stop because the strap was in the way. Her sex muscles kept tightening. She was tempted to lean over a little so maybe she'd be less aware of the butt plug.

He released her chin and unhooked the overhead chain from the collar. "Walk around. Get used to the feel."

She'd never get used to having both her holes distended. Instead, with every tentative step she took, her awareness of the twin invaders increased. The cuffs and collar were foreign, things done to her. In contrast, the dildo and plug felt as if they were part of her, an extension of her body.

With Master's steady stare propelling her, she slowly walked around the room, trying not to stimulate herself. The man and woman were still there but no longer locked together. The man now sat in the comfortable chair while the woman remained on her knees, her hands between her legs and in constant motion. Was that a slave's only reward, the opportunity to give herself some pleasure once her master had coated her face with his discharge?

Their relationship ceased to matter as she passed under one of the cameras. She was tempted to glare at it.

"You remind me of a horse wearing a saddle for the first time," Master said. He leaned against a wall. "You'd buck if you thought you could get away with it, but you can't, can you?"

She again looked down at herself, noting her still-red breasts and the contrast between her belly and the leather hugging it. "If I had use of my hands I could —"

"No you couldn't, because the harness is locked into place, same as the collar."

She stopped and bent her head to the left and right, trying to get used to what ringed her neck. Some men bought women gifts. This one had imprisoned her with a collar, handcuffed her, and *dressed* her in something resembling a chastity belt.

"I needed a key to work your previous collar. This one has an electronic locking device which means I don't need to be anywhere near you to manipulate it."

She wasn't sure what difference that made. Padded leather was one thing, designed as much for comfort as control, while this all-metal device made a single, undeniable message — domination.

Master's way of letting her know she belonged to him.

"One more comment," he said, "and then I'll let you experience. The tools I placed inside you work the same way — remote control."

Her legs tangled, causing her to stumble. She understood what he'd said and yet she didn't, the warning more than she could comprehend. Awareness of her too-full holes became even greater. The plugs and belt had made her clumsy. She could no longer take walking for granted.

"So," he continued, "it's time to demonstrate what I mean by remote control."

She sucked in her belly. "No, please."

"Oh, but yes. I don't know about you, but I'm going to enjoy myself."

He reached into a front pocket and withdrew a black device that fit in the palm of his hand. "Get ready for level one."

Level one coming from yesterday's electricity-powered vibrator had been pleasurable. However, things hadn't stayed like that for long and before Master had been done subjecting her to it she'd been a quivering mess.

A gentle vibration rocked her vaginal muscles. It felt good, whispery movements that slowly heated her and started her along a familiar journey. She, again, tried pressing her legs together to increase the contact, but the strap stopped her. Master had taught her what helpless stimulation felt like, so the lesson should be imbedded in her. Why, then, did the enforced sexual excitement seem so foreign? Thoughts of who might be watching snagged her attention. She was going to do something that should have been private but wasn't, maybe moan and cry and beg for mercy from a man prepared to watch her fall apart.

She wouldn't lose it. No matter what he put her through, she wouldn't.

Master held up the remote again and depressed a button. The dildo's speed increased and the butt plug started humming. She didn't know what to think or how to act. Like so many things that had happened since Master had captured her, she hadn't given approval, but it felt good. She settled her weight, locked her knees and tried to find something to look at, only to forget what she'd intended to do. Between the vibration and humming, everything was right and wonderful.

"I thought you'd like that." Master waved the remote at her. "What should I call it, all-consuming?" He frowned. "No, we haven't yet reached that point. Maybe I should take it up another notch. What do you think, ready for the next gear?"

The rocking, buzzing sensations spread through her. Her cheeks felt flushed and her lids fluttered. This was a beautiful place to be. "No, Master, not more."

"Why not? Don't tell me you're afraid of what's next?"

Was that a warning? He was telling her she'd hate it

when the vibrations became more intense? "No," she said although she wasn't sure that was the truth.

"Maybe. Maybe not. However, I'm not getting much out of watching you stand there like a statue."

She wasn't standing still, was she? It didn't feel like it, but then she was in no position to judge. Sexual pleasure, even if it included having something rammed into her ass, was wonderful. She didn't care that pins and needles still attacked her arms, or that she couldn't remember when she'd last eaten or gone to the bathroom. Floating had become everything.

"Your eyes are giving you away. Makes me envious thinking about what you're experiencing. Let's see if this gets me into the game."

They called football a game, but she'd watched enough to know it was much more than that. Master could be warning her, maybe preparing her, but for what?

This time when he lifted his arm, her legs trembled in anticipation.

Yes, more of everything. Humming in overdrive, her pussy jolting, afraid she'd fall. Top of her head threatening to explode. Dancing to an unwanted tune.

"For the record, you're about halfway to top speed. How's that working for you?"

If he expected her to answer, he was going to be disappointed, because he'd just tossed her into a whirlpool. Around and around she went.

Standing on widely splayed legs, she tried to reach the butt plug. She couldn't say what she would have done, whether she would have pulled it out, just that she hated being so helpless. She managed to hook her fingers over the leather belt. By turns she stared down at what little she could see of herself and locked gazes with Master.

Her pussy was melting while her sex juices ran over the dildo. In contrast, her nipples had become painfully hard. Her breasts shook without rhythm.

"That's never done anything for me," the other man said.

"If I'm not getting some benefit, why should I go to the effort of letting a slave get off?"

She wrenched free of what was taking place inside her long enough to notice that the man was getting out of the chair. He snapped his fingers at his slave and she scrambled to her feet.

"Let me know if anything interesting happens." He grabbed the naked woman's arm and shoved her toward the bathroom. "In the meantime, I'm going to park this one and go have a drink."

When the door closed behind the two, she continued to stare at it. She didn't want them back, but neither was she ready to be alone with Master.

"What's up?" he asked. "Missing your audience?"

He sat in the chair his fellow trainer had just vacated. With his arms on the armrests and his legs stretched out, it was as if he'd settled down for his own cocktail. While sipping on whatever drink the attentive bartender brought to him, he'd entertain himself by watching her, his little puppet.

Anger slammed into her. "The only thing I miss is my freedom. That's your doing."

When his eyes narrowed she knew she'd made a mistake. Just the same, she felt better, less like a robot.

The longer he stared at her, the more she longed to know what he was thinking. Now that she'd gotten past the worst of her disbelief over the turn her life had taken, the more she was able to focus on what he looked like. Tiny lines had formed at the outer edges of his eyes. There was a scar above his left eyebrow and another on his chin. She wondered if he resembled his parents and if they knew what he was doing. Did he have siblings, maybe brothers he'd fought with while growing up and sisters he'd protected from men who turned out to be too much like him?

"Freedom's relative," he said at length. "We all give up elements of self-determination."

"Not like this! How dare you try to justify your behavior by — "

"Shut up!"

The command jerked her back to reality. Then he flicked a glance at the camera, and for a moment, it was just the two of them.

Looking more resigned than angry, he aimed the remote at her. "You have so much to learn, so much you need to comprehend."

Energy pulsed through the intrusions. The sensations brought her onto her toes and threw back her head. There wasn't enough air in the room, no place to run to. Master became two-dimensional and she couldn't distinguish him from her surroundings. Need clawed at her, shook her, took her deep into herself.

She was still struggling to crawl on top of her fierce arousal when the vibrations became even more intense. She felt as if she was being thrown into space, falling, desperately grasping at something to hold onto, lost in pleasure.

Her knees buckled. Somehow, she wound up on her side on the floor, curled into an awkward fetal position.

"Coming, coming, coming! Oh, God, coming."

Shock after shock backed up in her. Her legs jabbed at nothing. She was being devoured from the inside, shaken into insensitivity, only to be hauled back into the firestorm of an unending climax.

"Make it stop. Please, make it stop!"

Seconds ticked by, every one lasting forever and yet over in a heartbeat. Even though she was certain she was dying, the death was glorious. She'd go out in a blaze of release, forever a slave to her body's need for pleasure.

"Master, Master, Master." She was vaguely aware that she was still on her side with her legs flailing and useless fingers trying to capture the air.

Master spoke again. As his incomprehensible words fell away, the tornado he was responsible for lessened so she no longer felt as if she was being shaken by a monstrous dog. She continued to come, but now there was less fear and more pleasure.

He kept her in subspace for a while before the things inside her backed down even more. She imagined herself on a cloud with a hot wind occasionally raking her. During those moments she wanted nothing else, and when the cloud broke apart and she started to implode, she wanted that too.

Nothing to do but experience.

No, not a cloud. The floor continued to support her and her limbs felt as if she'd been trying to rein in a massive horse. At least the horse had stopped running at full speed. Holding her breath, she tried to connect with her body. Little made sense beyond realizing she was no longer being torn apart.

"What's happening, slave? You still want me to make things stop?"

Sitting upright took every bit of strength she possessed. "It…"

He leaned forward. "Go on. What were you trying to say?"

She couldn't remember but couldn't simply admit that, not after what he'd done to her. The dildo and plug hadn't stopped humming, and sensitive as she was, she was certain she'd climax again if he kicked them up. She couldn't take it, could she?

Maybe.

Maybe worth dying for.

"You're a wreck," he told her. "Feel as if you've been in an accident, do you?"

She hadn't been in an accident, but she'd fallen off enough horses to have an idea what that would feel like — not good. In contrast, under Master's guidance and control she'd faced what it meant to be a sexual creature in ways she'd never known were possible. She didn't want another demonstration right now, couldn't take it, but soon — oh yes, soon.

At his hands.

She wrestled her spent body onto her knees and crawled

over to him. Being under Master's management wasn't something to fear after all. He'd given her a gift, taken her to a place where she'd never been but longed to spend the rest of her life in.

Thank you, she wanted to say except the words didn't go deep enough. Besides, the admission frightened her. She'd never had so few defenses. Even her father's violent death hadn't broken her into so many pieces.

No more thinking, no more trying to keep things together. This big man was everything, the only thing.

She leaned into him and pressed her breasts against his knees. "Master," she whispered, "Master."

He stroked her shoulder. "Always, or just for today?"

"I don't know."

"Neither do I," he whispered, and it occurred to her that he might be keeping his voice low so it wouldn't carry. "You're all right?"

Knowing he cared compelled her to rest the side of her head on his knees. His kneecaps were sharp. It didn't matter that she couldn't remain like this for long, she was here now, crouched before him as befitted a submissive and well-trained slave.

A deeply satisfied one.

Grateful.

Chapter Sixteen

"Look at it, smell it."

Tray's slave brought her nose to within an inch of his erection and inhaled, but her attention remained on him. Her earlier wariness had returned, but he didn't have to view yesterday's video to recall what she'd looked like then. The savage forced climaxes had left her shaking and wide-eyed, yet he suspected what she'd felt had gone deeper than helpless surrender. It hadn't been just a matter of him demonstrating what he could put her though, and her having no choice but to weather the hard lesson. She'd gone somewhere new yesterday, had briefly become someone she hadn't known existed.

Knowing he'd been the one to accomplish that made him feel powerful. Today he wouldn't mess things up by asking himself why the hell he was doing this. He'd come to the same decision about dildo and butt plug use, or rather non-use. Knowing they'd been in her had had him calling himself a bastard. Apparently there were limits even he wouldn't go beyond. As for how he'd react when, not if, management called him on it, hell, he'd consider that later.

"Think about having my cock in your mouth with the tip pressing against the back of your throat," he went on. "Imagine how it will taste and feel."

She hesitated, then, eyes bright, she extended her tongue and touched his rigid flesh.

What the hell? I didn't expect — "Why'd you do that?"

She rocked back and gazed up at him. Her dark eyes still glistened. "I don't know, Master."

"If you think you can get to me this way, you're wrong."

"That wasn't my intention."

Every time he thought he'd made progress with her, she said or did something that made him wonder if she was messing with his mind, instead of the other way around. Yesterday he'd been on top of things one hundred percent, but that was before they'd been apart long enough for her to have regained her equilibrium. Even though Robert and Cliff had warned him that would happen, he'd fooled himself into believing he knew her better than they did. *Yeah, right.*

"You've been brought to a party," he said. "Your owner commanded you to pleasure his guests. Tell me, what will you do?"

By way of answer, she gave his cock a pointed look. He supposed he should demand more. After all, this morning was supposed to be about taking her deeper into her new existence. The thing was, with her crouched between his gaping legs and his cock jutting from his unzipped jeans, he was hard-pressed to give a damn about lessons. With every hour she spent in his presence, she was becoming more complex, either that or her small, naked body was a lot more distracting than he'd anticipated.

Damn it, others were watching. He'd always pushed himself to exceed expectations and wouldn't stop now.

"Answer me, what are you expected to do at this party?"

"Please the guests."

"By doing what?"

Her hesitation made him wonder if she was debating defying him. Maybe she thought her submissiveness yesterday had altered the order of their relationship. He'd relished those moments when her head had rested on his knee, but that didn't mean he'd let her play him for a fool.

"It depends on what each man wants." She pushed her hair back from her face, careful not to touch the chain leading from her collar to his hand. "Some might want this—" Her lips brushed his cock's head, making him gasp. "Others might want something else."

Robert had encouraged him to reinforce this lesson with a switch applied to every part of her anatomy he could reach, but might that not be counter-productive? Too many whippings in rapid succession and she'd become immune to them, either that or constant punishment would leave her unable to think. That's why, other than the chain, he hadn't restrained her. He wanted her to experience a measure of freedom so she'd remember how it felt. Losing it would make a greater impact, wouldn't it? How had everything become so complicated?

"Master?"

Even with her hands on her thighs, her voice low and her breasts where he could easily abuse them, he had to work at thinking of her as his slave. "What?"

"Where do you go when you leave me? What is it like and will I ever see it?"

He yanked on the chain and pulled her off-balance until she threatened to crush his cock. She started to lift her hands but put them back on her thighs as he'd commanded earlier. Even with the distraction of having her so close, he admired her obedience. As for the reason behind it, he doubted it was because she was afraid of him. More likely she was testing both of their boundaries, which was something Carnal brass wouldn't allow.

More complications.

"You know you have no right asking." He shoved her back, only to regret putting so much distance between them. "These walls are your world. It'll remain like that until I decide to take you out of here."

"I can smell the ocean." Eyes moist, she studied him. "Do you go to the beach? Maybe you —"

He silenced her with a slap. No way would he let her emotions reach him. Yesterday, watching her twitch and come while not doing the same had been more than enough.

"So you want to feel sand between your toes, do you, slave?" He increased the tension on the chain. "Go on, let's see what you'll do to earn the right."

Her breasts rose and fell, her reactions reminding him of a horse balanced between trust and fear. She could wait for him to tip her one way or the other or make a decision.

Long seconds later, she lowered her head, scooted marginally closer, and opened her mouth. When Robert had said he'd wager that he'd have to beat her before she agreed to suck cock, he'd nearly taken Robert up on the bet. Looked like he should have.

Gripping the chain so hard the links pressed into his palm wasn't enough of a distraction, because as soon as her moist warmth surrounded him, his breath snagged. *Self-control,* Robert had repeatedly told him. *You have to stay in control. Otherwise, the bitches will smell your weakness.*

Hell, he wasn't weak. No one dared ever say that of him. What he was, was human, a mature man with a teenager's hard-on.

Eyes downcast and head bent, she took him deep into her mouth. No matter how much he tried to think of other things, he kept losing himself. His body was designed for rough use, not gentle touches. Women saw him as a damn Viking and he'd always risen to expectations. This — this was different. It took him to a quiet and yet exciting place. Sanded away some of the harsh edges he held his old man responsible for.

Yesterday, he'd locked his collar around her neck and tied her so she could barely move. He'd slapped and beaten her. He'd repeatedly forced her to climax. If the tables were turned, he'd want to kill the person who'd done those things to him.

Why then, was she willingly sucking and slurping? Why, with nothing more than his position of power working against her, was she treating him as if he mattered?

Would you stay here if you had a choice? Do you want to see where our relationship goes?

No way, he answered, prompted in large part by her now downcast eyes. If he mattered to her, wouldn't she still be looking at him?

Shutting down the part of him that wanted a connection between him and the clay he'd been charged with molding took work. Fortunately, his growing need helped tip the balance. Holding tightly to the chain, he sank back in the chair and let his eyes drift closed. Always before, having sex meant splitting his focus between his pleasure and his partner's. Now he could concentrate on himself.

"Keep it going. I want your hands on my thighs." He refilled his lungs. "Make me believe this is the only thing you want out of life."

Lightly holding his cock between her teeth, she leveled a gaze at him, and for a moment he believed in her. Then her eyes narrowed and she stared at his belly. Her palms settled on his thighs and she started massaging him there. Between the sensual movements and her sucking, he started sweating.

"Don't stop. Don't you dare damn stop."

This was good — the mountain nearly climbed and release only a step away. He rested his free hand on the top of her head. Damn, but being part of her jerking movements felt wonderful, a hell of a lot better than trying to pretend otherwise.

She sucked and drew back, bringing his cock with her, only to lean into him so it disappeared into her hot cave. Necessity seized him and he sat up straight and started slamming himself at her. She stopped moving, placed her hands against his groin, and offered herself to him. Applying equal pressure to the chain and her hair, he repeatedly thrust.

He was going down, falling into a familiar yet overwhelming vortex, lost as he'd been countless times before.

"Fuck, fuck, fuck." Arching off the chair, he started coming. She tried to draw back, but he held her in place while filling her mouth with his cum.

"Don't spit it out. Swallow it, fucking swallow it."

Finally, her strangled breaths got through to him enough

that he eased up on the pressure. His body still spasming, he stared at the whitish discharge leaking from the corners of her mouth.

He'd done it. Branded her with his fluids.

"Taste it, bitch." His mother would have disowned him if she'd heard him, while his old man probably would have declared him a stud. "Swallow it."

Although she studied him, he couldn't guess what she was thinking. His body was starting to relax and his cock had stopped throbbing, but he couldn't shut off his mind.

Both of their worlds had been turned on end. Before today, he'd given little thought to the possibility that he might change as a result of his new career. He should have gone deeper, looked closer at the ramifications of what he'd signed on to do. He also should have asked himself how he felt about such rules as those that dictated he teach her to see herself as a fuck toy.

Her hands returned to his thighs and she studied him without expression. Where had she gone emotionally, and did she give a damn what he was thinking?

"You made that too easy." Out of breath as he was, he should have waited before speaking. "Was the report on you wrong? Your skills include deep throating? This is nothing new to you, not something you have to be taught to do?"

She sank down a little. "Master, I don't know what you want me to say."

He looped the chain around her neck and held it with both hands, keeping her close and warm. "Oh, I think you do. The problem is you don't want to talk about it."

"I've performed fellatio," she whispered, "but I've never felt comfortable…"

"I find that hard to believe."

She briefly closed her eyes. Seeing the heavy links and collar around her slender neck wasn't helping his blood pressure, not that he minded. Having her naked all the time had stopped making the impact it'd had at first, but the contrast between the fragile column of her neck and what he used to restrain her was a kick in the cock. If they stayed like this much longer, he'd be ready for a second round.

"Why aren't you married? You wouldn't be here if you were."

Judging by her rapid blinking, he'd accomplished what he'd decided to do. He set the pace of her training. Her job consisted of taking every lesson to heart—and seeing him as all-powerful.

"What's wrong with you? Why doesn't a man want you?"

"You do," she whispered and slid her hands from his thighs to hers.

"That's what you think? Hell, you're just a piece of meat."

Pain flickered over her features. "Am I? If I mean so little to you, why is your cum on me?"

The cameras' microphones weren't particularly strong so it was possible no one would hear this conversation, but if he really wanted to have a private conversation with her, he'd have to take her elsewhere. Would she open up then, maybe tell him about her relationships?

Did he want to know?

Chapter Seventeen

"You're making things more complicated than they need to be. Training a sex slave is a simple process. Might equals right. That's all there is to it."

Marina had scrambled off the bed and knelt the moment the door had opened, but instead of it just being Master today, the man who'd helped Master capture her was here as well. Except for bringing her something to eat, she hadn't seen Master since yesterday when she'd given him oral sex. In some regards, she'd been grateful, because she wouldn't have known what to say or how to act if he brought up what had happened. At the same time, the solitary hours had eaten away at her sanity. Master had kept the small window open, making it impossible for her to dismiss the scent of sea air and sound of crashing waves. Why had he been so cruel?

Or was that consideration?

Leaving Master standing by the door, the other man approached her. "It's long past time for introductions," he said. "I'm Robert, Master Robert to you."

His voice had no inflection. Alarmed without knowing why, she tried to look past him to Master.

"Say it," he snapped.

"Master Robert." Hoping to forestall punishment, she lowered her head to the floor, even though she hated the increased sense of vulnerability.

"That's right, slave. From what I've seen, I know your trainer has taught you to view all men as your owners. He's been doing an admirable job of getting started with you, but I've decided to demonstrate some techniques. Pay attention. You can do that, can't you?"

Of course. She wasn't stupid. Hoping it was what he wanted, she lifted her head a little. "Yes, Master Robert."

He settled his hands on his hips. "Interesting. What do you call your trainer?"

"Master."

"Hmm. And if you were in a roomful of men would you still single him out?"

"Yes."

His gaze darkened. "That's your first slip-up. You forgot to properly address me."

This wasn't going to turn out well.

"One thing your trainer needs to improve on, and it's far from unique with new trainers, is how he relates to his slaves." He chuckled. "Or, more to the point, doesn't relate."

When he turned toward Master and held out his hand, Master pushed himself away from the wall and dropped the key to the chain that kept her fixed to the bed into his palm. Master didn't look at her.

"All right," Master Robert said after freeing her, "your first task is to crawl to the dresser and return with three pieces of rope."

When, even more nervous than earlier, she started to do as she'd been ordered, she broke into a sweat. Maybe they were laughing at how the chain trailed behind her leg. Master had allowed her to take a shower yesterday. Despite that, she felt dirty.

She had to stretch to reach the high drawer that held rope. The lengths felt so strong.

"Bring them back in your teeth."

Obviously one of Master Robert's intentions was to demean her. At least returning gave her a chance to study Master. Judging by the tight set to his mouth, he wasn't happy. As for why someone as imposing as Master would let another man take over — that was yet something else she had to try to figure out.

135

"She has learned a few things," Master Robert said as he yanked the ropes out of her mouth. "No doubt about it, your size is working for you."

"I don't need this," Master grumbled.

"That decision isn't up to you, me either. You did what your coaches told you to, right? Think of me as another team member, not management."

"Yeah, right. Are you going to tell me what you have in mind?"

"No. I want you to experience a bit of what she is." Master Robert grabbed her hair and pulled. She hurried to stand, careful to keep her hands off him. "I know you understand the benefits of keeping a trainee in the dark, but you need to internalize the concept. Watch."

For at least two days now, being in the same room with Master had kept her on sensual alert. In contrast, the moment Master Robert turned her from him and pulled her arms behind her, the only thing she wanted to do was run. His touches held no warmth. He tied her wrists then placed another rope around her waist and secured her wrists to the belt he'd created.

Being helpless wasn't anything new. She'd weathered it before and would do so now.

"You're looking at a basic fucking position," Master Robert said. "You can pull her forward like this" — he clasped her shoulders and forced her to bend over — "which puts her cunt within easy reach."

Master Robert rammed two fingers into her pussy from behind. She staggered forward. He prevented her from falling by snagging one of the rings on her collar. "Drape her over a handy chair and she's ready for use. The position obviously also works for back door action. Why don't you have her wearing a plug twenty-four-seven?"

"Because I don't."

"That's no answer."

"It's the only one I have. Look, I'm here as an independent contractor. As long as I get to the same place as everyone else, what difference does it make?"

As Master Robert hauled her upright and wiped his fingers on her buttocks, she all but tasted the tension between the two men.

"We've already had this out," Master Robert said. "At least we did as far as I'm concerned. There are rules we all have to comply with, standards —"

"I don't need a lecture. Let's get this done."

"Fine with me. One thing I'll hand you, you've shown her it won't do any good to fight."

If she hadn't been so nervous she would have laughed at the notion of trying to pit her strength against Master. Robert — she refused to think of him as 'Master' anymore — might have been a different story.

"How about you go stand where you were," Robert said to Master. "That way I can concentrate on one thing."

And not have to worry about Master overpowering him, she concluded. She just wished she dared think of Master as her protector.

When Master was again leaning against the wall, Robert pointed at the floor. "Down."

Hating Robert, she nevertheless did the only thing she could. In position before him, she noted his polished air, complete with expensive slacks and shoes and a designer shirt. His nails were professionally cared for and every hair was in place. He even smelled expensive. She preferred Master's earthy scent.

"This too," Robert said, "is a basic stance." He placed his fingers on either side of her mouth and pinched, forcing her to open it. "There's no reason for you to utter a word of explanation. Just tell her to get ready to deep throat you."

Robert was arrogant. To him she was a tool and not a human being. He'd never think to ask why she was unmarried.

"Keep your mouth like that, whore. At the moment that's the only part of your anatomy I give a damn about."

He unzipped his fly and pulled out a half-erect penis.

"There you go." He shrugged and flattened his hand over her mouth. "Nothing to it."

"Mechanical as hell," Master said.

And far different from what had happened between Master and her, her need to demonstrate her gratitude for her multi-orgasms had driven her to try to please him.

"What do I care whether she acts like a robot as long as she gets the job done?" Robert retorted. "Maybe that's your problem. You're looking for a personal connection between master and slave." Smiling a smile she'd have loved to have wiped off his face, he ran his finger around her gaping mouth. "Slaves learn dependency on their masters same as dogs learn not to bite the hand that feeds them."

Robert was being careful not to get his finger close to her teeth. Maybe biting him would be worth the punishment. At least she'd have a few seconds of victory before all hell broke around her.

"I have to hand it to you," Robert continued. He closed his fingers around her left nipple. "I've never mouth-fucked a slave without first installing a safety device this soon after training begins."

"I didn't have to."

Because I want to give you pleasure.

"You intimidate her. The problem is you've been relying on that intimidation instead focusing on the finer points. It's those points that potential owners are looking for."

"I don't agree with you," Master said, "but I'm willing to listen."

"You don't think she's scared of you?"

"She was at first. I'm not sure anymore."

"And that's a hell of a problem." Robert rolled her nipple about. "Besides, you're robbing yourself of a hell of a lot of fun."

He found pleasure in seeing a captive shake with fear while in his presence? How sick was that? Of course, she reminded herself, Master had started out the same way, hadn't he?

"Here's how I've always handled early sessions," Robert went on. "These techniques have worked here for longer than I've been on staff. Stick to the program and you won't have any trouble."

Robert had barely acknowledged her existence, which she knew was on purpose. "Keep that position," he said. "So much as twitch and you're going to rue this day."

She hardly cared that Robert was returning to the dresser, just that her nipple was free and he'd stopped testing her self-control. She still felt the imprint of his finger where it had circled her mouth.

"This is what I thought you'd use." Robert held up a metal and leather device. "Works off the principle of those things that keep car hoods up."

She risked a glance in Master's direction. It was almost as if he wished he wasn't here.

Sighing, she reluctantly turned back to Robert because she had no choice but to acknowledge what he now held up to her face. The O design was simple. All he had to do was position it inside her mouth and she wouldn't be able to bring her teeth together. Not only that, his cock would fit into the forced space.

"Usually I wouldn't say anything to a bitch at this point," he told Master. "However, I want to draw your attention to something. If you'll notice, I've done nothing to stimulate her. I could of course, and often do turn one on, but this time my intention is to set up a counterbalance of sorts. I'm going to get off by using her. All she can do is kneel there and take it. There won't be anything resembling a reward."

"Why not?" Master asked.

"Because I'm a bastard." Robert positioned the metal O over her mouth and shoved it into place. "A multi-talented bastard."

All too soon she understood what he was talking about. He drew out the process of preparing her to act as a receptacle for sex by taking more time than was necessary fastening the various leather straps. Afterward, he returned to the dresser and retrieved a thin, stiff switch.

Don't let either of them see your fear. Keep your helpless anger to yourself.

That turned out to be easier said than done, because Robert was a master manipulator. He waited until his cock was lodged in her mouth before starting to switch her. He repeatedly barked orders for her to stay still while stinging blows landed on nearly every inch of her body.

True, Master had beaten her, but he hadn't thrown his pleasure in her face while he'd been doing it. Robert obviously loved mixing things up and keeping her off balance. He laughed while he rammed himself down her throat and crisscrossed her flanks with lines of fire. He could have kept her in place by holding onto her hair or connecting a leash to her collar, but that would have been the simple way.

"You're dirt. Trash." Spittle landed in her hair. "Sagging breasts and a cunt covered in stubble. You smell like the back end of a horse."

The demeaning words lashed her almost as deeply as the whip did. She knew he was saying those things for effect, but the more he repeated them, the harder it became to rise above them.

"No wonder you're here. You don't deserve to be among the public. You aren't normal." The whip repeatedly stuck her breasts. "This is the only thing you're good for." He grabbed a fistful of hair and shoved her face against him, flattening her nose and filling her mouth.

Her world became a hazy red as he continued to deny her the ability to breathe. She tried to suck in air, but his cock took up too much room. No matter how much she struggled, he continued to force himself on her. Blow after blow rained on her hips and buttocks.

"Worthless whore. Stinking trash."

Come. Please come. Then let me go.

Either he couldn't guess her thoughts or he didn't care. She suspected it was the second. The beating intensified.

Was he angry at her and if so, why? Desperation banked inside her, making it impossible to think of anything else. Her head roared while the need for air made her sick.

Too far gone to consider the consequences, she threw herself to the side, twisting away as she did. She lost her balance and would have fallen if he'd let go of her hair. It didn't matter because suddenly she could breathe. Hanging helpless in his grip, she stared up at the man who'd turned into a monster. Even though she still couldn't see clearly, his smile made an impact. Garbled sounds erupted from her.

He stepped back, lifted a leg, and kneed her in the chest, releasing her hair as he did. The blow knocked her onto her back with her legs and arms trapped under her.

"That's how it's done." He stood over her and started in on her breasts with the whip. It didn't matter that he'd taken something off the blows, her breasts were on fire. Hating her existence, she flailed about like a bug caught in a spider's web. "Got it, do you? You're nothing, nothing."

"That's it, damn it!"

Master's voice barely penetrated. Even when he stepped into her line of sight, she didn't have enough left to think about him. Robert tapped her cheek with the whip, making it sting.

"I told you, that's enough!"

Suddenly Robert seemed to levitate. One moment he was looming over her, the next Master had grabbed him around the waist and lifted him. The whip clattered to the floor near her.

"What the hell are you doing?" Robert spluttered.

"Stopping something that should have never started."

Chapter Eighteen

"I don't care," Master said. "You can try to feed me that line of bull until hell freezes over and I'm not going to buy it. She could have been seriously hurt."

Marina knew better than to lift her head, but had studied her surroundings when Master had brought her in here. She'd noted three middle-aged men in leather recliners. Not long ago she'd been a quivering, silenced ball of misery in a room made for punishment and control. She wasn't deluded enough to think this might be an improvement, but at least this opulent room featured a picture window that faced the ocean. Maybe she could throw herself at the glass. Even if she cut herself to pieces, at least she'd die free.

"Robert would never damage valuable property," a man she couldn't see said. "He has too much of a stake in Carnal's finances."

"He'd lost control. Look at her. She's bleeding."

After untying her and removing the disgusting O gag, Master had told her to go into the bathroom. She'd been shaking so much that at first she'd been unable to focus on her image in the mirror. When she had, she'd wished she hadn't. A half-dozen thin cuts on her thighs and hips seeped blood. The outsides of both breasts were scratched, prompting her to gently wipe them with a cool, damp washcloth. Fortunately, she'd barely been cut there but bruising had begun.

Master hadn't come in with her, opting instead to continue arguing with Robert. Both men had cursed, but, although they'd been talking about her, she'd been unable to focus on what they'd been saying.

She'd still been in the bathroom when she'd heard a new voice. Master had ordered her to join Robert, a newcomer, and him. After she'd obeyed, he'd clipped a leash to her collar. The newcomer, the elegant woman she'd seen when she'd first been brought to the Carnal facility, had commanded her to turn in a circle. As she'd complied, the woman had taken pictures of her.

Now, not long after the woman had left, she, Master, and Robert were in the room with the massive window. Everyone else was sitting, while she'd been ordered to kneel. Master was behind her, his legs out of reach. Strangely, his presence comforted her.

"We'll have the cuts treated," the man who'd started the conversation said. "There won't be any scars."

"It didn't have to happen," Master countered. "She didn't do anything to deserve being treated like that."

"And your point is?" Robert snapped. "Tray, you know there doesn't always have to be a reason for punishing a slave."

"He's right," another of the men interjected. "You understood that going in. Robert's particularly good at the art of keeping a trainee off-balance, which leads to dependency."

That didn't make sense, not that anyone cared what she thought.

"She's my trainee. The rest of you signed off on her, which means any and all dependency she experiences should be directed at me."

"Until it's transferred to whoever buys her," the new speaker said. "Look, Tray, every trainer is granted a certain amount of leeway when it comes to technique. We asked Robert to provide a demonstration of a proven technique because we've seen signs of an inappropriate relationship between you and your subject."

"Inappropriate?"

"You want an explanation? All right, here it is. Dependency and emotional attachment are two distinctly different components. A slave must comprehend that a master provides everything, even the air she breathes. She becomes conditioned to turn to him for the most basic of needs and will do everything she possibly can to avoid his displeasure. She may be terrified of him, but she understands she needs him to stay alive. There's little room for hatred in that scenario."

The more she concentrated on what was being said, the more she wanted to be anywhere except here. Somehow, before she became too cowed to try, she'd escape.

"We don't want to see emotional attachment between trainer and trainee, because it complicates an owner's domination over his slave."

"I don't give a damn about her," Master said, "so don't go thinking I do."

At his words, pain stabbed her. She tried to tell herself that was what she wanted to hear from the man intent on changing her but couldn't.

"You might not believe you do, but you're human and you're working with another human being. Rest assured it's something we've all been through."

"That's right," Robert said. "Tray, right now you're thinking I'm a bastard because of how I worked her, but think of my technique as a necessary element in self-preservation. If you're going to be as successful at this as we believe you're capable of being, you *must* emotionally separate yourself from your trainees. In part that's accomplished by focusing on the various steps. You didn't think about your opponents' personal lives when you were facing them on the football field, right?"

"No. I didn't."

Was Master still looking at the naked and whip-striped ass she presented to him, or had he lost interest in her?

"Exactly. Training slaves isn't any different. You can't completely control how a slave sees you. Some become more emotionally attached to their trainers than others do. You'll learn to adjust your techniques to account for that.

The more you distance yourself from them the easier your job will be."

She didn't care who was talking. Surprised as she was because the men were saying what they were in her presence, she felt removed from it. Any day now she'd find a way to get free. In her mind's eye she envisioned herself racing naked and barefoot down the beach while Master pounded after her. His greater weight would slow him. She'd get away, hide somewhere until it got dark. She didn't care whether she had to stay awake all night as long as, come daylight, she was far from this horrible place.

Free.

Never to see Master again.

"Our intention isn't to belabor the point," one of the men said. "It's vital that any and all disagreements between Carnal staff members are resolved. Then we move on. Tray, how would you like to see this handled?"

When Master didn't immediately respond, she risked lifting her head and glancing back at him.

"I'm going to explain something I don't believe anyone in this room is aware of." For a moment he locked his gaze with her, then dismissed her. "The public sees football as a contest between aggressive men. To a large extent that's true, but behind the scenes we're, in essence, pawns. Owners have the final word in everything, including whether we go on working. Football was my life. It was the only thing I wanted to do."

"If I was built like you," a man said, "I would have made the same decision."

Master shook his head. "Maybe you wouldn't have if you understood the sacrifices. For me..." When he looked at her again the others ceased to exist, but then the moment ended. "There's more to me—and to every man who puts on a uniform—than a physical body. I wanted to get a certain someone to notice me. Putting on that uniform was how I chose to try to accomplish that."

Had he succeeded? His tone and somber expression made

her wonder if he hadn't.

"My years of being paid handsomely for my services in exchange for giving up the right to say who I worked for, under what circumstances and for how long are behind me." Simply by planting his hands on the chair arm and sitting straighter, he became even larger.

"I'm going to make mistakes, but I pride myself on being a quick study. Go ahead and offer suggestions about how I can improve my performance. I know I have a lot to learn. Just keep your hands off her."

Because you want me to yourself?

She paid little attention to what was said after that. Maybe it didn't matter, because not long after, Master pulled her to her feet and led her out of the room.

"That's it," he said when they were in the hall leading to the space that had become her world. "It's back to being you and me."

She wouldn't be alone. For as long as Master chose to keep her with him, her life would revolve around something other than earning a living at a career fraught with danger, a career that could end with a single spill.

"Master, thank you."

He stopped so abruptly she nearly ran into him. "For what?"

"Saving me from —"

"You aren't saved. Don't you get it?"

Her hands burned with the need to touch him. "Anything's better than having Robert —"

"Don't be so sure."

Chapter Nineteen

The trainee hadn't objected when he'd ordered her to sit in the chair designed for restraint and stimulation. Despite Carnal management's insistence that her cuts and bruises were no reason to suspend her training, he'd pretty much left her alone for three days after Robert had laid into her. This morning's examination had assured him that she was basically healed, due in large part to the cream he'd been given.

Three days and nights of minimal contact had helped him as well, not that he'd ever tell her. Against advice, he'd given her reading material and had set up a TV. He'd spent some of his time surf fishing but had also worked out and gotten caught up on sports news. He'd commented on some posts his sister had left on her Facebook page and responded to the email from his mother. There'd been nothing from his father, and he hadn't bothered sending him one.

As he strapped down his slave's arms and legs, he compared her leery expression to his sister's wide grin on her Facebook page. If anyone did this to Sara, he'd kill the bastard.

Then why are you —

"You were too independent," he told her. Anything to silence questions he didn't want to ask, let alone try to answer. "We men are simple creatures. All a lot of us want from women is a little consideration."

A shudder sent her breasts into motion. Thinking to get her to concentrate on today's lesson, he secured her collar to the chair's high back.

"Not all women pay for that lack or perceived lack of

consideration, but you obviously pissed off the wrong men, men determined not to let you get away with it."

"They had no right."

She hadn't spoken since he'd walked in, which must be why her voice distracted him from tightening the waist restraints. He'd have to look closely to see the whip marks and, fortunately, no longer had to apply medication to them.

"Right has nothing to do with it. You are where you are."

"You're responsible for this, not them."

He'd been warned not to allow a slave to get lippy, so why was he allowing her to get away with it? "I could argue with you, but I'm not in the mood." He positioned one of the horizontal straps fixed to the restraint chair over her upper arms just above her breasts. "It's time for yet another demonstration of what your body can be made to do."

Eyes wide, she looked down at herself while he tightened the strap so it compressed her breasts. The chair had been designed to keep a slave's legs widely spread, with the opening in the seat directly below her crotch. He probably hadn't needed to strap down her ankles, calves, and thighs, but studying the contrast between her muscled legs and three wide black strips of leather, he was glad he had. The more effort he put into getting her ready for action, the better. She was becoming dehumanized, which was what he needed to have happen if he hoped to reach his goal.

His sick goal.

No! He had to find a way to stop such thoughts from intruding.

She could no longer move. There wasn't a part of her body he hadn't restrained in some way. Granted, she could still talk, but he could change that at any time. For now, however, he needed to pull more out of her. Leave her with even less she could call her own.

A few days ago he might have filled her in on what he intended to do, but if there was one thing he'd learned from that debacle with Robert, it was to proceed with confidence.

Otherwise, those judging his performance might spot or believe they'd spotted a weakness. She might too.

He pulled the device designed to plug a slave's holes from under the chair so she couldn't see what he was doing. She strained to swivel around toward him but only succeeded in tightening her bonds. He'd already taken the case containing the various dildos and butt plugs out of the dresser so it would be within reach.

"You're going to tell me some things." He opened the case. "No matter what's happening to you, I expect you to answer my questions."

"What questions? You already know everything about me."

He didn't know nearly enough. Leaving her to worry about what he might or might not say next, he set out the various tools. They screwed into the base and could be electronically lifted into place and set into motion. He chose a medium-sized dildo and a plug marginally larger than the one she'd worn the other day.

After securing them to the base, he slid everything back under the chair. Still kneeling, he used the remote control to start the invaders moving upward. When they touched her, he stopped the motion so he could manually open her butt hole. He watched the pre-lubed plug disappear into her. Her toes curled and she lifted her heels off the floor. Otherwise, nothing moved.

"Now for—" he started, only to shut up. Damn it, not telegraphing his intentions was harder than he'd told himself it would be. Surely it wasn't because he was still taking pity on her. He'd gotten past that, right? Everything from now on was about—about what?

Why did these lapses keep happening? After all those years spent learning from an uncaring bastard he should have had the technique down.

"Why?" she asked. "That's what I'll never understand, why you do things like this."

The air seemed to swirl around him. He was caught in

an unanticipated tornado with bits and pieces of himself slamming into each other. Hadn't he put his years as a well-paid indentured servant behind him? He thought he had. Now he wasn't sure he'd ever get to that point. That's what the damn tornado was all about — the truth demanding to be acknowledged and him not wanting it to happen.

The plug was in place, buried in her and waiting to be put to use. Next would come the dildo then he could watch her *suffer* — make her talk. As soon as he touched her sex lips in preparation for drawing them apart, he encountered moisture. He collected a little and placed his fingers under her nose.

"You want to explain this. What have you been doing when you're by yourself?"

"Nothing, Master. I haven't touched — "

"Spontaneous excitement?"

Her head drooped a little, stopped by her restrained neck.

"I'm serious, slave. Give me an explanation."

The way her lids started to close, he thought she was trying to separate herself from him. Then she seemed to gather strength. Even constrained the way she was, he remembered how she'd appeared as her horse had trotted into the winner's circle, head high and back proud.

"I have a woman's body," she said. "It responds in ways I don't always understand."

"And what is it responding to right now? We haven't gotten started."

"Haven't we?" She tried to look down at herself. "Maybe this is anticipation."

Not dread but eagerness, interesting. "Are you saying you want this?" He again reached for her labia.

"Yes," she muttered.

Most slaves didn't admit to their sexual weaknesses so soon — at least that's what he'd been told.

"Then I won't disappoint you."

She made no attempt to move as he slipped the dildo into her. Like the plug, it had come pre-lubed, but thanks to her body's juices, that turned out not to be necessary.

How would she react if it was his cock?

In anticipation of what today might require of him, he'd masturbated last night. He could have made use of one of the complex's slaves, but that would entail some measure of communication and he hadn't felt up to it — not with someone he didn't give a damn about.

He gave a damn about the trainee who'd once been Marina? Wanted this to be good for her?

Sick to death of questions without answers, he positioned the recliner across from her, with some six feet between them. He sat and clicked on the remote. She shivered then slowly relaxed. Her features gentled and, judging by how she kept staring at him, she wanted him to comprehend what she was going through. Both intrusions were working her at the lowest setting. The first time he'd stimulated her, she'd remained tense throughout. The contrast between that and today was interesting, much like a once wild horse that had come to associate humans with food and gentle grooming.

He debated asking her to describe what she was experiencing but didn't want to engage her in conversation — hell, today wasn't going to include a dialogue. He was here to learn what he could about her while sharing nothing.

After giving her the better part of a minute to get used to the low gear, he switched to second. This time she didn't shudder. Instead, she smiled and rested the back of her head on the chair. He hadn't shaved her since that first time, and a faint dusting of hair drew his attention to her pubic area. From where he was sitting, he couldn't see everything of her sex or what was being done to it, but he could imagine. The imagining fed his erection.

She *was* enjoying herself — of that he had no doubt. From what he could tell, she wasn't hampered by dread that pain might accompany the pleasure. Maybe she'd found a way to lock herself in the moment. He wished he could do the same, because it seemed as if he was always looking down the road, seeking more, incapable of simply accepting that the present was good.

He gave her another minute before turning things up another notch. Her breasts started jiggling, as did her inner thighs. Her hands opened and closed, her toes curled and her lashes fluttered.

"Good," she muttered. "Yes, good."

"But will it remain like that?"

With an effort, she focused on him. "Don't play games."

"Don't play games, please, Master."

Judging by how her mouth twitched, she didn't know whether to laugh or be afraid. "Thank you, Master. No matter what happens later, I need this."

"Because?"

She tried to reach for her crotch. Her chest heaved. "Because it's all I have."

You bastard. You damn bastard.

"Not today it isn't," he said. "I'm going to give you some tasks."

This time there was no mistaking her anxiety. At the same time, he clearly saw her effort to remain on top of her sexual responses. He came close to assuring her that he didn't intend to punish her, but if he did, he'd have to answer to management. Better to keep them as off-balance as he was doing to her.

"Why aren't you married? We talked about that the other day, but I didn't get an answer."

She again extended her fingers toward her crotch. He tried to imagine what unrelenting sexual stimulation would feel like, but he'd always gone straight to satisfaction. There was no need to engage in protracted foreplay when his sex partners fell all over themselves in their determination to please him.

"Marriage—it hasn't been important to me. My career is."

You career was important. "But being a jockey isn't something you can do until you're old enough for social security. What about a balanced life?"

Her mouth had stayed open. When she tried to shake her head, he guessed she was trying to clear it. Not touching himself was becoming damn hard. He hadn't wanted to participate until he'd gotten her close to her sexual edge. Was she there yet?

"I know — I know my jockeying days are limited but..."

"But what?"

"I have a — plan. A dream."

Not 'had' but 'have'. Self-disgust threatened to swamp him. "What is it?"

She stared at something beyond him. "It will take money — money I hope to earn as a jockey." She panted. "I want to teach people about horses — and provide a home for unwanted horses."

Her plan was so damn simple on the surface, but horse rescue was a money pit and giving riding lessons far from a high ticket enterprise. Still, from what he knew of her determination, she'd succeed if anyone could.

Or rather, she'd had a shot before he'd ripped her away from her world.

"It's a noble but selfish plan."

"What? How can you say that?"

She was again forgetting to call him Master, but they'd deal with her lapses later. "It would take all your time. There wouldn't be room for a husband or children."

Her head sagged. She repeatedly tried to lift herself off the chair.

"What's the matter, slave? Things getting rough for you?"

Instead of answering, she started tightening and relaxing her thigh muscles. He let her try to deal with unrelenting stimulation for a while, before kicking things up another gear.

"Not fair," she whimpered. "So not fair."

"Oh, I believe I'm being more than fair. In fact, I'm downright generous, because according to the Carnal manual you aren't close to deserving pleasure."

"Pleasure?" She redoubled her efforts to get away. "How

153

long..."

How long did he intend to keep her like this? He didn't know. Now that he'd set his plan to get her to spill her soul to him in motion, he wasn't sure it was what he wanted. Carnal existed to produce expertly trained sex slaves. No one gave a damn about their backgrounds or what dreams and desires they'd once had.

"This can't be a new experience," he said as he settled back. "You have a collection of sex toys."

Her lids kept fluttering as she struggled to focus on him. He concluded she'd split herself into two parts, with one aware of him while the more primitive half tried to deal with nonstop vibrations.

"My— They're nothing like this."

Of course they weren't. Batteries were hardly on a par with something powered by electricity.

"How often do you play with yourself, slave? Maybe you're so good at it that you have no need for a man. Is that why you sleep alone, because you have a satisfactory alternative?"

"No," she whispered. "No."

He couldn't say how he knew something had changed inside her. "Would you rather have a partner, maybe even a husband?"

Her eyes closed and she stopped trying to fuck the dildo and plug. "I don't know. I—I'm not very good at getting close to a man."

He stood and positioned himself between her widespread legs so he could finger her breasts. Instead of abusing them as he was expected to do, he kept the contact gentle. "Is it that? Maybe you keep men at arm's length."

"Maybe." She opened her eyes and locked her gaze on him.

"Why? Are you afraid of them?"

"No." Her chest heaved. "Everything's been different— since my father died. I don't know..."

"What don't you know?"

154

She started to take a deep breath, only to slowly exhale. Maybe she'd just now realized what he was doing to her breasts and didn't know how to deal with it. "Maybe—oh, God—whether I can trust one."

What the hell kind of a relationship had the two of them had? If the old man had raped his teenage daughter, it was a good thing the bastard was dead because he might have killed him. Some lines were never crossed, never.

Then what the hell about this one?

"It isn't—isn't what you think." The words pushed past lips she was trying to keep closed.

"Tell me what it was."

Chapter Twenty

She looked so close to tears he had to fight the urge to comfort her. He compromised by massaging her breasts. When goosebumps spread over them, he stepped closer so their thighs touched. She blinked and her eyes cleared. When he pressed the palm of his hand over her heart, she sighed. A second later tension seized her. Her mouth hung open and her legs shook.

"I can't—I can't come."

Maybe it was her admission that brought him back to reality. He could keep her suspended between pleasure and hunger and experience some of the same himself, but wasn't that counterproductive? Better to dig the truth out of her while she could still think.

Better to concentrate on his job.

"Tell me about your father."

The story came from her, one halting sentence at a time. The whole time he lightly massaged her breasts while her heartbeats pulsed through his fingers. After her mother's death from cancer, her father had stopped driving trucks and gone to work at a large-scale beef cattle operation. Father and daughter had moved into a mobile home on the acreage and, with Marina trotting beside him, he'd worked the long hours that were part of the ranching lifestyle. When Marina had been old enough for school, she'd had to take a nearly two-hour bus ride. Her friends had come from ranching families, but she'd spent most of her free time with her father.

Horses had become her passion. She'd ridden bareback, mothered the foals, learned how to treat many injuries, and several times sat beside dying horses with their heads on her lap. Her father had felt the same way about anything that lived. Yes, he'd taken responsibility for beef cattle destined for slaughter but he'd done everything he could to make their lives as pleasant as possible.

Father and daughter had been on the same wavelength. They hadn't needed to talk about their relationship, they lived it. Whoever got to the trailer first started dinner. They'd shared chores, listened to the same country and western music, and had gone to rodeos and horse races together.

"One day—he was using a tractor to move some equipment." Her eyes had become glassy and her body occasionally jerked. "It—" She shook her head but still looked mostly out of it. "I can't think."

"Yes, you can. You need to do this."

"Maybe," she muttered. "It had been raining and the ground was soft." She sighed. "The tractor tipped over. It landed on top of him."

Until now she'd been fighting to speak despite the vibrations wracking her body, but as she talked about the last day of her father's life, she seemed to separate herself from her reality. Her soft words were matter-of-fact. In contrast, her expression left no doubt of her emotional pain.

"Did you see it happen?" He'd continued to stand over her while she told him his story. His hands hadn't left her breasts, but he wasn't sure she was still aware of his presence.

"No." She twitched and her muscles remained tight. "He, ah, I was working with a horse. God—I—if he yelled for me I didn't hear him."

"You found him?"

Her eyes were both vacant and too big. "I don't know how long—he didn't die right away."

She didn't know how long her father had been under the tractor before she'd found him. Unsure whether it was better to change the subject or let her continue, he planted his hands on her thighs and leaned even closer. "I hope to hell you didn't blame yourself."

She blinked repeatedly, straining to get off the chair as she did. Maybe he was wrong but he wanted to believe she was trying to reach for him. At times like this a person, even a sex slave, needed to be comforted.

Her lips trembled. "I knew he was working on the side of the hill. It wasn't the first time the tractor had tipped over. I should have—"

He started rubbing her arms. Goosebumps came to life under his touch. "Don't. He knew the risks. You can't blame yourself. It won't change anything."

She was looking everywhere but at him, making him wonder if she was trying to separate herself from his words—from him. "I mean it. It wasn't your fault."

When she tried to shake her head, he cupped her chin. He pressed his other hand against her chest. "Your father wouldn't want you feeling this way. He was a good man."

"He was," she whispered. "Strong and kind. Gentle, so gentle. He didn't need much, just the weather co-operating. That's what he always said—if he was going to pay his bills and earn his keep and never get in trouble, the least the weather gods could do was reward him."

"He also wanted his daughter to live her life."

The moment he spoke, he knew he'd said the wrong thing, at least as far as Carnal Incorporated was concerned. Fighting the part of him that wanted to remain with her, he back-stepped to where he'd left the remote and aimed it at her. For years he'd seen the opposing team members as the enemy. That's what this woman was, someone to be mastered and walked away from. Mostly walk away from when he was done with her.

"I don't need anything more from you today," he told her. "You've spilled enough guts for one day, revealed enough vulnerabilities."

Watching her try to regain her composure, he stopped lying to himself. Whatever she was, she wasn't his enemy.

He thought about explaining that his intention had been to take her beyond losing her father, but he was in uncharted territory. Not only didn't he dare forget about the ever-present cameras, he couldn't fathom what someone went through when they spotted their beloved parent's broken body.

"My father means nothing to you." She stared fixedly at the remote, as if challenging him. "You don't give a damn what happened to him. This is all part of your sick plan to break me."

A kick in the nuts couldn't have wounded him more. His first impulse was to push the vibrators as high as they'd go and let her deal with the consequences of her outburst, but she deserved better.

"I do care about your father," he told her as he turned things off. Instead of hurrying into an explanation of why he'd said what he had, he watched. At first she remained tense, then she started to relax. She draped her fingers over the end of the chair arms.

"Do you want me to beg, Master? Plead with you to let me climax? Where's your whip? Aren't you going to—?"

"Stop it." He dropped the remote to the floor and returned to her. Barely believing what he was doing, he knelt before her and laced his fingers with hers. "I know why you're saying what you are. I got too close. Stripped away your layers. The only way you can put your defenses back up is by seeing me as your opponent."

"That's what you are." She didn't try to free her fingers.

Yeah, I know. "That isn't the point. Your world revolved around your father and when he died, a part of you died with him."

Master was right. In some regards, Marina had felt half alive ever since that horrible day. It had been the sudden loss, having her father one moment and nothing the next. She'd been so young when her mother had died that she hadn't really mourned her. In aching contrast, she'd been a teenager when fate had robbed her of her only parent. No matter how many times people told her not to hold herself responsible for the accident, she had.

"I was wrong," he said. "I don't want you to stop talking after all. You said it had been raining and the ground was muddy. Was it spring?"

Her body still pulsed. If she wasn't careful, she might tell him how desperately she still needed to climax. "Spring. A Saturday morning."

"And you were, what, off somewhere?"

Do it. Just get it over with. "I'd slept in. As soon as I got dressed, I hurried outside and told Dad I was ready to help him. He, ah, the night before we'd talked about the garden we wanted to plant. We'd decided to devote the morning to getting the ground ready."

"And he wasn't happy when you overslept."

"No, he wasn't." Master's fingers were so large they spread hers wide, but without the contact, she wouldn't have been able to go on. "I kept telling him I was sorry. He said it was all right but I knew it wasn't."

"Why not?"

"There's so much that has to be done in the spring. He'd just planted hay and needed to mend some fences. The calf auction was coming up. Part-time employees were on their way to help us. Our agreement had been to— I'd promised I'd do the preliminary tractor work if he'd help me set the rows for what I wanted to plant."

"Your father let you run the tractor?"

She couldn't remember when she'd last felt like laughing, but she did now. "I'd been doing it for years. I was supposed to be on it that morning."

"If you'd been driving, you might have been killed."

"No," she whispered, "because I would have been working north of where he was. We hadn't seen eye to eye about where to put the garden. When I didn't show up on time, he decided to do it his way."

"So there was tension between the two of you. Did that

happen often?"

She tried to shake her head. Feeling the collar tighten brought her back to reality. She pressed her fingers against his, which was the only way she could let him know him she didn't want this contact after all. He slipped his hand free, stood, unhooked the collar, and released the strap around her shoulders. Renewed blood flow ran through her.

"Talk now," he said. "You and your old man were at odds that morning."

"Don't call him that." Expecting punishment, she warily studied him. "He was my father."

"You're lucky. Not all of us feel that way."

As far as she could remember, this was the first thing of a personal nature he'd told her. So much had changed between them today. It might not last, but she was hungry for anything that made her feel less like an object.

"I know," she said. "Dad and I hardly ever argued. I apologized and he said it was all right, but I knew it wasn't because he was under so much pressure."

"Teenagers need a lot of sleep."

"It didn't matter. I was expected to carry my weight. I'd been making some money working with horses people didn't have time for, so decided I'd try to make it up to Dad by gentling a gelding so I could return it to its owner and get paid. The gelding had a lot of energy. I started by letting it run. By the time I got back…"

Chapter Twenty-One

"How long did you have nightmares?"

He'd known that about her. "Too long."

"What happened then? Who finished raising you?"

People didn't have conversations like this, not when one had stripped, restrained and forcefully stimulated the other, not when one of them had her holes stuffed while the other stood over her looking like a conquering warrior. Just the same, she needed to continue.

"No one." Had she already told him that? It didn't matter. "Dad and I were the only ones living on the property. The owner—he had some health issues and needed to be close to town—let me stay."

"By yourself." Master stretched out hands that had already done countless things to her and started rubbing her shoulders. "It was just you in that trailer, then."

She nodded and hurried to explain that the owner had promoted one of the ranch hands to take her father's place. She'd continued to care for the ranch's horses and any calves that had needed special attention. During calving season, she'd spent more time in the barn than in her own room. She didn't tell Master that spending a night curled around a calf was easier than listening to the empty trailer creak.

As when she'd told him about life before her father's death, Master had said little. Maybe that's why so much poured out of her—and maybe she was laying herself out to him because her pussy was no longer out of control and he stood over her.

Still massaging her arms with his thighs touching hers

and his eyes — his eyes saying what?

"I think I know why you haven't allowed a man to get close enough to ask you to marry him."

His low tone, and what he'd said, caught her unawares.

"For a while," he continued, "I figured it was because no man could measure up to the pedestal you'd put your father on. He was your everything."

"He was. A good, good man."

"I know." He brushed her cheek.

Do that again, please. I need to be touched like that.

"I could tell you he was human, point out that he could have handled things better with you that last morning, but it doesn't matter."

Master's voice continued to caress her. Her eyes burned.

"What matters is that his dying scarred you. It hurt so much, caused you so much pain."

He pressed his hands against her cheeks and steadied her head.

"It's all right if you cry."

"No," she whispered, afraid and hungry all at once. "Not after all this time."

"The years don't matter if the wounds haven't healed. I know what pain feels like, but I haven't gone through what you have. I can't fathom a sense of loss so deep you're afraid to take chances again."

"I don't want to be hurt." Was she really saying this, and to him of all people? "Not like that, ever again."

"But you're robbing yourself of a full life."

His mouth was so close and her emotions so raw. Stretching, she parted her lips. After a moment, he leaned over and pressed his mouth to hers. Something she'd never experienced washed through her. She felt newborn. She seemed to be floating, moving effortlessly through space, sharing that space with a powerful, gentle and exciting man. A small part of her insisted she wouldn't be doing this if she was thinking straight, but she desperately needed human contact — this contact — with him.

His mouth still locked with hers, he unfastened her arm restraints. At first she couldn't think how to make them move. She tried to warn herself to keep them where they were, but they took on a will of their own and wrapped themselves around his solid neck. He could break free, of course, punish her for touching him without permission, but she'd deal with the consequences later.

For now, she'd hold on to her captor, her master, the man who understood so much about her. That should have been enough, a seeking out, a tentative journey. Why then, were her lips against his and why, when he opened his mouth, did she do the same?

She'd been cold and he was offering warmth. After all those days and nights of being afraid, this man had come to comfort her.

When, a long moment later, he pulled back, she reluctantly let him go. His expression unreadable and body tense, he released the rest of her restraints and picked up the discarded remote.

"Tell me something," he said. "Should I remove the intrusions or start them working again?"

Pleasure me. Take me into myself. Make this all about me. "I don't know —"

"Are you afraid?"

"Not of you," she told him when not long ago that would have been a lie.

"Yourself, then?"

No! She wasn't going to admit that. "This isn't real." She reached between her legs and fingered the dildo where it disappeared into her. She could have stood and freed herself — but did she want to? "Artificial."

He touched the remote. First the butt plug then the dildo slid out of her. Returning his stare, she fingered her labia. The air smelled of the sea and female arousal. Master's erection threatened to rip his jeans.

Not believing this was her, she stood on shaky legs and planted herself before the domineering and dominant man.

Watching for his reaction, she unsnapped his jeans and lowered the zipper. After drawing his cock through the slit in his briefs, she cradled him in sweating, unsteady hands. Maybe he expected her to kneel and perform oral sex, but she needed more. Needed something she didn't have words for.

He cupped his hands around hers, which increased the pressure on his cock. She extended her fingers and ran her nails over his scrotum.

"Careful," he warned.

"I'd never —"

His chuckle stopped her. She no longer felt as if she might explode. These moments were good, something between equals. When he placed his hands on her shoulders, she turned her attention to exploring his cock. He'd been circumcised, and she relished gliding her fingers over his length. Maybe what he'd placed inside her caused her quick, hard responses, but maybe she was simply reacting like any woman would in the presence of a sexy male. Whatever the reason, if there was one, she dipped her head so she could study what she was doing.

His cock was larger than any she'd seen, the weight in her palms more potent. This part of him could rule her. She'd never get enough of it, would want it in her always. Was that it, she pondered, as his fingers traveled from her shoulders to her swollen and sensitive breasts? She'd become a sex addict around him. She'd never get enough, constantly rub against him to get his attention. They'd have sex five, six times a day and when they weren't they'd — they'd talk. Get to know each other. Bind their lives together.

Shocked at the notion that she might willingly stay with him, she froze. However, her hands remained on him and despite her sudden chill her pussy remained hot — hot and alive.

"What is it?" he asked.

"So much — I never thought I'd..."

He ran his hands under her breasts and lifted them so her

nipples pointed at his chest. "Neither did I, but I'm going for it."

She should have known what he meant but didn't begin to put it together until he'd stepped back from her, stripped off his clothes and sprawled on his chair with his legs outstretched and his cock putting her in mind of a thick, living spear. She could have tried to get away, but not only wouldn't she have gotten far, she wanted to stay where she was.

No, she corrected herself as she continued to study him. She couldn't remain in place any more than she could deny how much she'd revealed about her life short minutes ago.

"This might be your only time for self-determination." He took hold of his cock and angled it toward her crotch. "What's it going to be?"

She couldn't remember whether he'd called her slave today. Neither could she say whether she'd referred to him as Master, but words weren't the only thing that had changed between them. He was telling her to direct the next step in their relationship. She had no window into the future, no way of knowing whether she'd go back to being his chained possession, nothing except need and what she'd revealed about the emptiness inside her.

One shuddering wave after another threatened to swamp her as she closed in on him. When she was so close she could make out the individual hairs framing his sex, she placed her hands on his knees. Two cameras were trained on her front while two more recorded her backside. If Tray — right now she'd think of him as a man and not a master — didn't care who saw, she'd meet him courage for courage.

Eyes downcast, hoping to keep her swirling thoughts private, she trailed her fingers over his thighs. Muscles, hard as stone, tightened. He let go of himself and placed his hands behind his head, but the position didn't fool her. He was no more relaxed than she was.

Do it. Step beyond yourself. Take what might be the greatest risk of your life.

Propelled by the command, she climbed onto the chair, straddled his hips, and lowered herself onto him. Her flooded pussy absorbed him. Sighing, he closed his hands around her waist. She braced herself on his shoulders and settled onto her knees, taking him deeper as she did. This felt so much better than the dildo had, superior to every other cock she'd had in her.

She struggled to find something to say but couldn't pull her thoughts together enough for a word. He bucked off the chair. The movement resonated throughout her. For a few seconds, she believed that being on top said something new about their relationship, but as his eyes darkened, the question of where this was going no longer mattered.

"Show me what you're capable of," he challenged. "Fuck like a liberated woman."

Not a slave. Embracing the lie, she repeatedly rose and sank down. She concentrated on keeping her inner muscles tight, going faster and faster while sweat ran between her breasts. He slid a hand around her waist and pressed his fingers into the small of her back, keeping her in place and allowing her the only freedom she needed.

He started slapping her wildly shaking breasts, making her cry out in delight. She arched her back, thrust her arms behind her and anchored herself by digging her fingers into where his knees and thighs joined.

She moved machine-like, shaking until she felt as if she was falling apart. Her head became heavy. Her breasts flailed so he sometimes missed slapping them.

"Fucking." She hissed, "Yes, fucking you."

"Who am I? Go on, say it!"

She didn't know what he wanted, didn't know anything except that this inner fire was going to kill her.

"Say it!" A blow almost hard enough to knock her to the side made her breast burn.

"Master. You're my master."

"My slave's fucking me," he threw at her.

He struck her other breast three times in rapid succession,

and she growled with each blow. He pulled her forward then pushed her back. Each time he did, it changed where his cock pressed against her sex walls. The storm attacking her grew, her hair flew about so she could hardly see and sweat now coated her legs and trickled down her back. Still she kept fucking him, driven by a force she didn't try to understand.

This might be the only thing they'd ever share. She'd dive into the middle of it and become a fuck machine, scream sometimes, sob and moan.

And burn. Mostly burn.

A thunderclap sounded as the first wave of her climax struck her. Wild with excitement, she gaped at the hazy features of the man who'd brought her to this place.

"Yes! Oh shit, yes!"

He pulled her down on top of him, holding her prisoner with his greater strength as he exploded inside her.

She didn't care whether this was what he'd wanted. Only riding the incredible waves that threatened to stop her heart mattered.

Finally, though, she had nothing left to give. Her body had spent itself, leaving her so far gone she lacked the strength to sit upright. Besides, Master hadn't released her.

His cock slowly shrank. They were still united, but she stopped feeling as if they shared a single heart. Her thoughts turned to the unseen ocean and she again imagined she was drifting in the waves.

Then, even though she fought it, she acknowledged that she was again thinking of him as her master. Hiding from reality wouldn't change it, so she sat up and looked down at him. His eyes slowly focused on her.

"We're not going to talk about this," he said.

"No," she whispered, "we aren't, Master."

Chapter Twenty-Two

Tray closed the door to his private quarters behind him and walked over to the window so he could study a stretch of beach cluttered with driftwood. When he'd gone out there the other day, he'd taken pictures of tall, slim grasses and wild flowers that grew among the bleached wood. He'd had no idea what he'd do with the images he'd captured with his smartphone, but the contrast between what was living and dead had caught his attention.

Today he couldn't remember why he'd spent so much time out there. He attributed part of his mood to the fact that he'd recently gotten off and wanted to get some sleep. However, he wasn't sure he'd be able to fall asleep, let alone stay there.

Too much had happened, too many words shared, emotions hauled out and stripped naked. Granted, most of that had been on her part, but he'd come close to opening up about himself.

Damn close.

He'd just left the slave when Robert had appeared in the hall to inform him that management wanted to talk to him. He'd told Robert he wasn't interested in being called on the carpet.

"Fucking a slave's hardly against the rules," he'd insisted. "Just because my methods are unorthodox doesn't mean they were wrong."

The moment Robert had again issued the *invitation*, he'd told Robert to tell the others to go to hell. He knew what he was doing and expected to be left alone.

He'd gotten the solitude he'd demanded. Unfortunately,

he wasn't as sure of himself as he wanted everyone to think.

Why had he kissed her?

That's what it all boiled down to, wasn't it, he acknowledged as he watched several seagulls float with the air currents. Despite what he'd promised her about not raping her, no one would have protested if he had. In fact, forced sex was part of the training process. He wouldn't have been surprised if management had taken bets on when he'd fuck her. On the other hand, he guessed the last thing they'd expected was him locking his lips with a slave in training.

That wasn't all he'd done, damn it. He'd guided her through the story of her father's death and how that death had impacted her. She'd lost her rudder after her father died. He'd been the standard by which she measured all other men. None had met her exacting, unrealistic and yet understandable standards.

She'd spent the intervening years trying to protect herself from more of the pain that had nearly killed her. If she didn't love someone she couldn't be hurt.

Toughen up, boy. I don't care how old you are, I don't ever want to see you cry. A real man's as hard on the inside as he is on the outside, got it?

His old man's words and the slap that had accompanied them echoed through him. He couldn't remember how old he'd been the first time he'd heard them, maybe five or six. The refrain had become an almost daily utterance until he'd learned how to lock his emotions away. Toughening up hadn't won him his father's love, but at least the old man had acknowledged a grudging respect for the son who'd taken his hard edge onto the football field. Over time Tray had realized the bastard had no business being a father, but by then the lessons had stuck. More than stuck, he'd been able to parlay them into a man's career.

That wouldn't change now.

* * * *

170

Marina hadn't reacted when Master had tied her hands in front, hauled her out of her room and into the one occupied by the other slave she shared the bathroom with. Not seeing Master for nearly a day had given her time to regain her emotional balance. She should never have told him about losing her father. It was too late to take back the words, but she'd do everything within her power to prevent something like that from happening again. It wasn't as if she'd cared about Master when they'd kissed. Considering what she'd been subjected to, it was understandable that she'd needed even a hint of humanity from someone. Never again.

She was a slave in training, a woman awaiting her chance to escape.

The other slave had already been secured in the middle of the room with her arms over her head and a large red ball gag filling her mouth.

"I'm glad you decided your subject's ready for a little group education," Cliff said as he handed Master an identical gag. "Seeing themselves mirrored in another slave makes an impact."

"It wouldn't have occurred to me until I saw that tape last night." Master hauled her within inches of him and jammed the rubber ball against her lips. Much as she hated doing so, she obediently opened her mouth. "Quite educational."

"That they are. Hey, I'm impressed," Cliff said as Master secured the gag. "My bitch still resists when I silence her."

"Does she?" Master ran his hand over Marina's stretched skin. "Guess this one knows better."

At least he hadn't called her a bitch. However, neither had he given any indication that he was thinking about the precious, fragile, and dangerous moments between them yesterday. She obediently stood where he indicated. Neither did she resist when he hoisted her arms over her head and secured her to the same long beam the other slave was tied to. Today was all about locking herself away. She'd take whatever punishment and pleasure Master inflicted on her. She might not be able to hold back from reacting to a whip or vibrator, but that's all it would be—her body doing what instinct demanded.

The lesson, not that either man spelled out their reasons for what they were doing, began with a warming up that called for a slender leather cat-o'-nine-tails being applied to nearly every inch of hers and the other woman's bodies. Master commanded her to turn in circles while he flicked her with the multi-strands. They stung more than hurt. Every blow kept her flesh alive. What she could see of her body was almost uniformly reddened. Her nipples hardened so they stood out as if begging for attention. He struck her there, of course, but gave equal attention to her arms, legs and buttocks. Much as she hated rotating to make things easy for him, she had no choice. At the same time, her thoughts kept locking on a simple and yet complex phrase—pain and pleasure.

When would this punishment end and her reward, if that's what it was, begin?

His expression, or rather lack of one, didn't change. He didn't look into her eyes, focusing instead on painting her where he wanted her painted. Every time she faced him, she vowed not to try to back away, but her feet had minds of their own. Unfortunately, she had no place to go and no idea when this would end. Sweat coated every inch of her and her stretched body begged for relief as he snapped his fingers and held up his hand. As she complied with his unspoken command, she thought back to teaching horses to stop via pressure on the reins. She would have never beaten one.

"Let's see if they're adequately warmed up," Cliff said. "It doesn't take much to get my bitch going anymore, but yours hasn't had as much time for the behavior modification to have sunk in."

"I'm curious myself." Master draped the whip over her shoulder.

He planted himself close so her sensitive nipples pressed against his middle and pushed back on her shoulders, lifting her off her feet. He'd moved to the side by the time she swung into place. He pushed again. Back and forth she went. No matter that she dragged her feet on the floor, he easily kept her in motion. Her arms bore her full weight, the strain making them burn. The same heat reached her crotch.

"Interesting." He planted his splayed hand on her chest and brought her to a halt. "I turned her into a living swing."

Cliff had been doing the same to his slave. "I get a kick out of demonstrating control in unique ways." He ran a hand between the other woman's legs. The way his hand was angled, Marina guessed he'd placed a finger inside her. "Well what do you know? Her system's still in perfect working order. It's amazing what a little tuning can accomplish. How about your bitch?"

The way Master sucked in a breath, she wondered if he'd order Cliff to clean up his language, but after a moment, he slipped both hands between her legs and pressed against her inner thighs. She had no choice but to spread her legs until she was standing on her toes.

Master was again dominating her body, turning it into his plaything, his experiment. She told herself she didn't exist for his pleasure, but was it a lie? After all, he ruled everything about their so-called relationship.

Not just their relationship, what made her a woman.

He didn't immediately check her pussy for moisture and each second thrummed through her. She was waiting for Master, waiting to be touched, stimulation building, knowing what was coming, unable to hurry things along.

"How about it, slave?" Master asked. "Think your body's going to be honest today?"

It would because she had no control over it. He knew that, just as he knew countless other things about her, including the sorrow and guilt at her father's death that she still held in her heart.

Anxious waiting ended the instant he cupped his broad hand over her pussy. She entered a new existence. He no longer pushed on the insides of her thighs, but it made no difference, because his hand kept her from closing her legs. He lifted her off the ground. Even with him cradling her, she started to tip back. Her tethered arms prevented her from completely losing her balance. She hung where he'd hoisted her, with her legs dangling on either side of his muscled arms.

"It'd be a lie if you told me I'm not one hundred percent in charge," he said. "Good thing you're gagged. This way you aren't tempted to insist you have any say in the matter. And for the record, Cliff, my palm's sticky."

She'd been aware of her sexual heat from the moment Master had come for her, but it had taken second place to first the whipping, followed by being turned into a human swing, followed by this unnerving demonstration of his strength. Master had done those things just as he'd do everything else he wanted to her.

"What about it, slave? Are you ready to get down to business?"

She nodded.

"Because?"

Memories from yesterday swamped her. When she'd crawled on top of Master and welcomed his cock into her hungry core, he'd fulfilled her in ways she'd never experienced. She'd felt complete, cherished even. Bold and submissive at the same time. Free and a slave to her woman-needs. She keenly remembered how fucking him had allowed her to dismiss her burning legs and the collar's reality. How she'd spun mindlessly into a volcano. A volcano she longed to return to today.

Trusting he'd understand her message, she squeezed his hand as best she could while gazing at where his legs joined. His erection sent a message that needed no explanation.

"My slave's getting pretty good at wordless communication," he said as he let her down. She stood on hot, uncertain legs.

"That's a vital skill for someone wearing a gag and unable

to use arm gestures," Cliff replied. "I hope you don't have any issues with watching someone else get it on, because I've been waiting long enough. You're more than welcome to stay."

"I intend to. Like you said, a slave better understands her situation if she sees it being played out in someone else."

By the time Master released the rope holding her arms over her head, Cliff had already hauled his slave over to the bed and was tying her spread-eagled to it. He'd placed a pillow under her buttocks so her sex was accessible to him. The slave looked both apprehensive and eager.

Master untied her wrists and re-secured them behind her. He then again fastened her to the overhead apparatus and pulled up so she was forced to lean over. After positioning her to his liking, he showed her a three-foot long leg spreader. Dehumanized as she felt as he put it on her, she kept reminding herself that he was getting her ready for sex.

Sex. The one thing that gave her new life meaning.

Cliff had removed his slave's gag. As a result, Marina knew the moment the other woman started responding to the cock now planted deep inside her. The sounds she made were part whimper and part pleasure, inhuman.

Master cupped the hand that had been against her sex over her gag. She tasted her excitement. Should she thank him for taking the ball out of her mouth? Maybe she shouldn't say anything until he gave her permission to — if she could remain silent once he was inside her.

Unfortunately, he left the gag in place and offered no explanation as he stood in front of her and pulled down his jeans. The instant she saw his erect cock, it became her world. Moaning into the ball, she strained toward him.

"A well-trained filly." He patted her cheeks. "That's what you're becoming, little slave. An obedient and eager-to-please piece of property."

He was wrong! She'd never —

Never what, demean herself? But she already had.

Repeatedly.

Self-disgust warred with the fire he'd lit in her. She managed not to hang her head as he moved behind her and planted his hands on her buttocks. She somehow kept from pushing back in invitation.

"You're a slut." He eased several fingers over her throbbing labia. "You're even more a slave to your sexual needs than you are to my cock. You don't care what goes in you here, just that something does. As long as you're like this, you're fair game for any master. You'll grovel, demean yourself."

Not just any master, she longed to tell him, but if she did he might believe only he could control and mold her, when that wasn't the truth.

Wasn't it?

"The first time I saw you, the term 'wild child' came to mind." He pressed his fingers along her slit. "That's because I saw a comparison between you and the horses you were riding. You were fearless. I love riding. The feel of all that gentle power has always made an impression on me. My problem is I need a horse that can handle my weight. No racehorse for me. You get — got — speed. I get sturdy."

He'd mentioned something about having been around horses before. If she'd been capable of thinking of anything except what she prayed was about to happen, she'd pull the bits and pieces of what she knew together for a clearer picture. She'd also find the courage to deal with his use of the past tense when it came to her riding horses.

Thinking would have to wait until he was done with her. Until she'd reached saturation.

Master took advantage of her inability to move by bringing her to the edge of sexual release, only to pull her back. He repeatedly finger-fucked her while her garbled pleas took on a life of their own. A touch to her clit stole her breath. She hated being so transparent, but her body wanted what it wanted. Drool trailed from her forced-open mouth and she bucked helplessly in her restraints, both fighting and worshipping this man.

All too soon, the only thing she wanted from life was him, not just his cock but the whole of him. What did it matter if she'd once been a wild child? He'd tamed her, broken her.

Finally, his cock plowed into her with a fierce strength that sent her forward the few inches her bonds allowed. A whimpered 'thank you' morphed into a scream. Caught. Helpless. Wanting and scared. Drowning and being born.

She couldn't fuck him as she had yesterday. This time it was all his doing and she was his dancing, climaxing puppet. Much as she loved the hot release, futility threatened to swamp her. There was no stopping her rutting master. She'd become his sex doll, his prisoner and slave.

His.

Chapter Twenty-Three

"Remarkable, isn't it?" Robert said. "That's what keeps me here. Every slave is different, and yet they're fundamentally the same." He chuckled. "I liken them to bowling pins. Sooner or later they're going to get knocked over."

Tray chuckled. "I've never bowled."

"Okay, you come up with an analogy. I don't give a damn."

The better part of a month had passed since he'd captured this, his first slave. In that time, she'd gone from taking freedom for granted to accepting that her master was in charge of everything about her existence. He'd done what he considered a good job of going by the Carnal rule book while taking her through the necessary steps. Several times management had criticized his performance, with regards to the use of punishment techniques, but he'd told them in no uncertain terms that he didn't believe in pain for pain's sake. To his way of thinking, he made much more progress via liberal doses of pleasure. She might not have agreed, because he pretty much kept her on sexual overload. She occasionally begged him to stop pushing her into one climax after another, but the benefits in terms of his getting laid were worth it. Someone looking at their relationship from the outside would conclude that they couldn't get enough of each other.

That might have been true of him because, hell, he loved watching her react to being stimulated. As for her—that's where things got fuzzy.

He'd spent considerable time trying to analyze what she'd experienced in that month, but although he now understood more than he thought he ever would about the female psyche, he still had a lot to learn. He'd also acknowledged he'd probably never know everything about her.

Come tomorrow, he reminded himself, *it won't matter.*

"At first I compared her to a horse because her job called for being around them," he said, from where he sat to Robert's right. Other trainers were here, carrying on casual conversations while they sipped whiskey and watched the events in the adjacent room. "The first time I saw her I saw a wild child, independent. But that's changed so much I'm no longer sure what she is."

Robert shook his head. "The fundamentals are still there. If a master knows what he's doing, he'll have a compliant little sex slave, but if he lets up or handles her wrong, he'll have a damn wild animal on his hands."

The thought of some man mishandling the slave he'd spent a long, draining month getting ready for tomorrow's auction angered him, but he wouldn't let his emotions show. Fortunately, thanks to his childhood, he knew how to do that.

"So once she's been paid for, I'll no longer have a say in—"

"None. She'll be shipped off to wherever her new owner wants." Robert lightly punched his shoulder. "What you're feeling isn't unique. After all the time you've spent with her, of course you feel a certain connection. There's nothing like taking on a new project to get over this one. You must be getting tired of handling the same boobs and pussy. Time to move on."

As he studied the half-dozen slaves through the one-way glass, he wasn't sure how he felt, beyond a sense of loss at knowing his time dominating her was coming to an end. Despite his doubts about this job, and he had a number of them, he loved being in control.

In preparation for taking the females out of isolation in advance of the auction, they'd been brought into the same room. However, this was hardly a friendly get-together. All but one was gagged, two — including his — wore nipple clamps. Each was restrained in some way.

He'd thought management had lost their damn minds when they'd told him how to prepare her. The strap around her elbows that kept her in a perpetually arched position looked flat out wrong.

No, he corrected, not wrong. The problem was he was weary of questioning Carnal's techniques. They worked all right, worked fantastically. He just needed to get that through his thick skull. Case in point, his slave had become a near nympho. All he had to do was sexually stimulate her, inflict a little pain, or order her to service him and her juices started flowing. If he'd been this good at training horses, who knew how his life might have turned out.

"Tomorrow's the last day these bitches are going to see each other," Robert said. "They know it and yet they'll try to bond. Watch. You'll see what I'm talking about."

Other than her collar, the elbow strap, nipple clamps, and gag were the only things his slave wore. She could bend her elbows and lift her lower arms, not that it did her much good because she couldn't reach the gag, let alone the wide leather band that kept her in the unnatural position.

Next to some of the slaves who wore hobbles or had been fastened to hooks, she had freedom of movement. Earlier, she'd approached one who'd been forced onto her toes with her arms chained over her head and had awkwardly patted her. Now she was near a tall, thin woman who couldn't move, thanks to the pussy hook anchoring her to the ceiling. In addition, that woman's arms had been stretched out to the sides and fastened to the wall behind her. As inventive as that restraint was, Tray was more interested in what his slave was trying to do. The pussy hook woman was the only one who hadn't been gagged. She was asking his slave questions. His slave responded by nodding or shaking her head, and sometimes trying to speak.

"What's that about?" he asked Robert. "Why should

they give a damn about the other captives when they know they're *graduating* tomorrow? Besides, this isn't communication by any stretch of the imagination."

"Call it mutual support. Did your slave resist when you pulled her arms back?"

He took a sip of his drink, but instead of the liquor relaxing him, he felt even more on edge. "Her muscles tensed, but she knows better than to put up a fight."

"And you love seeing her submit."

"You know the answer to that."

"I sure as hell do." Robert laughed loud enough that the other men looked at him. "I'm wondering what might happen if she gets some dried-up old bastard for an owner. After being trained by you, I wouldn't be surprised if she pushes the limits."

His tension kicked up another notch. "What'll happen if she does?"

"Depends on the bastard, but it won't be good. My guess is the first time she tries to run will be her last."

Could her master cripple her, make it impossible for her to ever run again? The thought made him sick to his stomach.

Tray finished his drink in a single swallow and held up his empty glass. A naked slave with large gold nipple rings hurried to fill his order. He hooked his little finger through the ring and pulled her to her knees in front of him. Smiling, she held onto the whiskey bottle with one hand while rubbing his cock through his jeans.

There was no need for his slave's new owner to cripple her, he told himself despite the delicious distraction. He'd thoroughly trained her to put her master's pleasure first.

At least he hoped to hell he had.

"Ah," someone sitting behind him said, "here come the vultures."

He was debating whether to ask Robert how trainers viewed buyers when the door to the slaves' holding room opened and two strangers walked in. Judging by their demeanor, Tray concluded they knew each other. Maybe they were repeat Carnal customers.

Within a couple of minutes nine other men joined them. Interesting. He hadn't expected there to be more potential buyers than slaves.

Having to share the room with these self-assured men was the last thing they wanted to do, not that they had a choice. Growing up, he'd attended a number of livestock auctions and had expected something like that to take place here.

The slaves were being manhandled, that pretty much summed it up. Two beefy middle-aged men had planted themselves before the slave with the pussy hook in her and were taking turns slapping her breasts. Every time she started to turn away, the hook pulled her up short. One of the men grabbed hold of the rope attaching the hook to the ceiling. Mouth open, she stood on the tips of her toes. Judging by the men's grins, he guessed she was begging them to take mercy on her.

Disgusted with the heavy-set men, he searched the crowded room for his slave. He finally spotted her in a far corner, where she was being led in a tight circle by the chain between her breasts. The muscles in her forearms strained as she tried to reach the nipple clamps. The man making her trot looked to be in his forties. He was barely any taller than her, with narrow shoulders, wide hips, and a swollen cock that stuck out from his green slacks. His shirt was an even brighter green, his damned shoes white. What hair he had was so long it reached his collar. How the hell could this loser afford to buy a slave?

"Who's he?" he asked, pointing. "Those clothes are a joke."

"He calls himself Rafer. He's rebelling against his old man, Mr. Conservative. This is the third time he's been here. Now that his old man had a stroke and he took over the company, I'm guessing he finally has the money to spend on his idea of a toy."

The longer Tray watched Rafer the more the bastard

disgusted him. The man stopped pulling Marina in a circle and switched to pulling up and down on the chain so she had to repeatedly kneel and scramble to her feet. Even from this distance he knew she was frightened. As a result of the intense sexual conditioning he'd put her though, she might also be excited, but maybe not.

Years ago he'd been afraid of his old man. During those times when fear had loosened his bowels, he hadn't been able to begin to put his mind to how to get into the bastard's good graces. He'd stammered and begged to be forgiven. It hadn't mattered whether he'd messed up or not, he'd apologized.

Tray guzzled his second drink and signaled for a third but didn't drink it. If he wasn't careful he'd shatter the glass because he was holding it so tightly.

"This part's hard," Robert said. "Every trainer gets to the point where he believes he's found the right balance with his slave. He's onto her wavelength. He knows her strengths and weaknesses. Having to watch someone without a clue about what goes on between her ears or in her pussy sucks."

"He's a bastard."

Robert jerked his head, indicating the other room. "Most of the men in there are bastards. If you're going to stay in this business you have to get used to it. Put her behind you. Move on. Take what you learned from your first time and build on it. First time's the hardest. After a while you'll get into a rhythm. My suggestion, let it happen."

Countless coaches had told him to learn from every game, quarter, and play so he figured he knew what Robert was talking about. Truth was, spending so much time with his slave had drained him in ways he hadn't expected. It wasn't just how his body responded to her naked body and not always being able to satisfy those needs. The emotional component was equally, if not more draining.

Yin and yang. Positive and negative.

He wouldn't immediately sign up for another trainee.

Instead he'd take a few weeks off, maybe go to regional horse races, maybe look into buying some acreage and getting a few horses. A lot of people wound up with buyers' remorse when they realized how much owning a hay burner cost. He might offer to take a few nags off their owners' hands and get them for free or next to free. Show the bastard of a sperm donor that he hadn't bought the argument that horses weren't worth the powder to blow them up.

That was it, he'd turn the spread he had yet to buy into an unwanted horse sanctuary, do something good for something else for a change. Invite his old man over to see it.

As another trainer behind him cursed, he shut down the crazy thought, but not before admitting that his slave was at least partly responsible for his thinking. He'd never tell anyone, of course, but maybe offering a home for a horse no one wanted would turn out to be his way of atoning for robbing her of the life she'd planned.

"You bored?" Robert asked. "Maybe you're thinking about riding her one more time before turning the reins over to someone else."

On the brink of telling Robert to shut up, he realized the other man was deliberately forcing him to face what tomorrow entailed. Robert was right. Along with his slave's physical body, he'd be surrendering the notes he'd taken throughout her training. Her new owner would know where she'd come from, what had happened to her parents, and that she'd been a damn good jockey. He'd also know she loved the smell of the ocean — and might use that information to make her life pure hell.

He downed his drink, barely noticing the burn in his throat before looking for her. Rafer had brought her close to the one-way glass. Her attention was locked on Rafer, yet he wondered if she suspected she and the others were under surveillance. He wouldn't be surprised if she couldn't concentrate on anything except what was happening to her.

He was the last person on her mind.

Too bad it didn't work both ways. Tonight, tomorrow, and the foreseeable future would be a hell of a lot easier if she hadn't crawled so far into him—and if training her hadn't satisfied him in so many ways.

"She's going to go for a shitload of money," Robert observed. "Some of these slaves are pretty far gone. They're little more than pussies, mouths, and asses. For whatever reason, she still has spark."

He hadn't spent much time with the other trainees so couldn't compare her to them. In some regards he felt sorry for her, because that spark might make her future even less bearable, and yet he was glad she was still alive in the ways that counted. Their so-called sexual relationship hadn't been uninhibited. How could it be when no matter how turned on she might be, she could never forget the essential difference between them? Much as he'd liked having an always-available sex partner, and he sure as hell did, the reality was she wasn't willingly in this. Come tomorrow, it might become even less so for her.

In an attempt to shut down his damnable mind, he focused on the just out of reach action. Rafer was removing her gag.

"That's allowed?" he asked Robert.

"We don't put many restrictions on men with money. There's limits, of course, which is why we're watching."

There wouldn't be any limits left once she belonged to someone else. Watching Rafer force her to her knees and use his nipple-hold to drag her against his cock, he resigned himself to the fact that just about anything and everything was allowed today. Eyes nearly closed, she opened her mouth. Instead of immediately plunging into her, however, Rafer draped the chain over his cock. Her fingers opened and closed spasmodically, proof that having her breasts pulled up like that hurt.

He had to hand it to her. Despite her obvious discomfort, she remained in place as the bastard filled her mouth. She tried to keep her movements slow and measured but Rafer was having none of that, evidenced by how he repeatedly slapped her cheeks.

Damn it, for most of the month he'd been training the slave, he'd shut down the pain once they'd started fucking. Even when he'd forced her into sexual frenzy, he'd stopped the punishment part so she could focus on what her body was capable of experiencing. That approach, he'd concluded, was how the dominant member of a master–slave relationship kept the submissive one under control.

Rafer with his stupid-ass outfit was going at it all wrong. No way would she get any pleasure out of this — but maybe that's what Rafer intended.

"I know what you're thinking," Robert said. "There's no tradeoff for her. Why would she want to please a bastard who can't be bothered to let her get off? Unfortunately, all we can do is try to explain to buyers how things work best. Once they're out of here, they can do whatever damn thing they want to."

Fortunately for the slave, Rafer had a hair trigger. White slime started dribbling out of her mouth. As soon as the bastard finished doing his thing, he rammed his shoe into her chest and sent her sprawling. Tray started to stand.

"Don't," Robert warned. "He has every right."

Another man positioned himself over her and, using her hair for leverage, hauled her to her feet. Rafer said something, only to have the newcomer wave him off.

"She's fair game," Robert explained. "These events remind me of dogs fighting over bones. Usually these bastards are too civilized to resort to fighting, but, when it happens, it can get crazy funny."

Several other trainers agreed. As the conversation turned to an incident last year that had resulted in two potential buyers being shown the door, he forced himself to watch. The slaves were overwhelmed, but that wasn't all. This preview was designed to give the men the opportunity to determine what the slaves were capable of. As a result, equal amounts of pain and sexual stimulation became the order of the day. The slaves stood their ground as fingers were rammed inside them. One after another they started responding, accompanied by laughter and catcalls from their male audience.

He wasn't sure how he felt when his slave spread her legs and repeatedly flexed her knees in an attempt to get off on the fingers lodged in her. Knowing her as he did, he knew the instant she started climaxing. If not for the lessons he'd taught her, she probably wouldn't have lost control. On the other hand, the fifty-something man was handling her like a pro. Pulling on her hair had hurt, but since then he'd been gentle — all except for keeping the nipple clamps in place and the strap around her elbows.

His slave might transfer her affection from him to this new owner. No longer would she study him with hunger in her eyes. Another man might get her to open up about her past. Another man would talk to her about the impact her father's death had had on her.

Disgusted with what he told himself were his booze-fuzzed thoughts, he stood and walked out. Instead of going to his room or the in-house bar, he headed outside. The moment the salty air reached his lungs the alcohol in his system started to dissipate.

Robert had told him not to be surprised if tonight's action didn't turn him on, but it hadn't. There hadn't been a single minute when he'd wanted to join in.

Maybe he wouldn't spend some of the money he'd saved during his playing years of acreage after all. Land would tie him down, to say nothing of how much work having horses took. Becoming a horse rescuer was crazy thinking. He didn't need the responsibility.

What he needed was time to himself, maybe deep sea fishing. He hadn't been to a football game since last year's playoffs. He could call some friends and see if they wanted to go with him. A lot of his former teammates were married with families, but a few like him were still single.

Yes, that's what he'd do. Get away. Reassess.

As soon as he did one more thing.

Chapter Twenty-Four

No matter that she'd stood in the shower until it ran out of hot water, Marina still felt dirty. She wasn't sure how many men had manhandled her, but then she wasn't interested in reliving the experience. Her shoulders and nipples and pussy ached. Brushing her teeth twice hadn't completely cleansed her mouth of a taste she wanted no part of.

At least she was alone and no one had seen the tears she'd shed in the shower, she reminded herself as she toweled off. It was dark outside, which was just as well because otherwise the need to be anywhere other than here would have driven her crazy.

After hanging the towel back up, she returned to her room and studied what she might never see again while fingering the collar Master had placed on her. She'd hated being locked in here, and yet thanks to Master, she'd learned a great deal about herself. Most of her education had been of a sexual nature and tonight she likened herself to a well-trained horse. At the sound of a starting gun she'd leap from the gate and gallop full out.

She sat on the side of her bed, spread her legs, and studied what she could see of her sex. It was still puffy from use and baby-soft because she'd shaved herself this morning at Master's direction.

Where was he? Someone else had returned her to her room, removed her restraints, and told her to clean up — as if she'd needed the reminder. She hadn't seen Master since early afternoon, which was just as well because he'd been short-tempered and had acted as if he could hardly wait to get away from her. Back then she hadn't understood why he'd ordered her to shave her sex and shampoo her hair with lavender scented shampoo. Now she did.

One of the men who'd pawed her tonight might own her tomorrow.

Shuddering, she stood and walked over to the window. Even though she couldn't jump high enough to see out, she again tried. Her weary legs barely got her off the floor. Fighting a sob, she returned to the bed.

Don't think. Just exist.

However, that was as impossible as falling asleep. She wasn't sure who she was anymore and that bothered her more than anything else. Being in a constant state of sexual arousal shouldn't be everything. She once been — been what?

Looking around did no good, because everything about the room reminded her of her transformation. The TV had been removed while she was being *inspected.* She'd stopped reading the newspaper Master had supplied because she felt disconnected from what was going on in the world. She'd sometimes tried to escape her new reality by revisiting her past or imagining what she'd do with her life if she were rich, but that had proved too painful.

She didn't always want to escape. In fact, much of the time she'd happily accepted the experience she'd been thrust into. Countless hours of everything revolving around sensual sensation had taken her down a road she hadn't known existed. Master had become her everything. He'd orchestrated the tempo of her days and nights, what she did, tasted, smelled, saw, felt, even thought.

All that would change tomorrow. It might turn out to be a nightmare, but until she knew for sure, she'd hold onto a thread of hope that whoever bought her was kind.

Life without Master? She couldn't fathom it.

She'd draped a blanket over her shoulders and was debating sitting in Master's recliner when the door opened. Her heart raced, her skin became sensitive and her nipples hardened at the sight of the big man who'd anchored her world for weeks. She couldn't take her gaze off his sober expression long enough to do more than note what he carried. He barely acknowledged her before handing her the bag.

"Open it."

Wondering if he cared that her hands shook, she unzipped it and pulled out a red and silver football jersey with the number thirty-eight on it and white cotton shorts with an elastic waist.

"Put them on."

What's going to happen? Why are you doing this?

Still shaking, she placed the blanket on the floor and stepped into the shorts. Wearing something felt strange, wrong even. The garments were part of his world and not anything a sex slave would be required to wear, but she wouldn't ask for an explanation. When she pulled the jersey over her head, she realized it was so long it covered the shorts and the neckline threatened to slide off her shoulder. Had it been Master's? Looking down at herself, she saw nothing of the sexual creature she'd become.

"We're going outside," he told her. "It's cool."

Outside? Had he really said that?

Yes, he had, she acknowledged, as a few minutes later he descended the stairs that led to the beach with her behind him. She was still shivering, now as much from the impossible thing she was doing as being in his presence. His minimal explanation didn't help, but it didn't matter as much as damp, salty air on her cheeks did. She was barefoot. When they reached the beach, sand warmed by the day seeped between her toes. It took everything she had not to drop to her knees and pick up a handful of what represented freedom to her tonight.

"Let's walk," he said.

Thankfully, he slowed his stride so she could keep up. She guessed he hadn't given her shoes so she wouldn't be inclined to run. Maybe she should tell him that was the last thing she wanted to do, at least until she understood more.

The moon was just coming up, but thanks to the solar lights around the stairs and in the sand beyond the tide's reach, she wasn't concerned she'd step on something sharp. The beach stretching out ahead and behind looked as if it had been swept clean. Between the surreal setting and the heat of the man now walking beside her she could barely think.

"This is the only way I can talk to you in private," he said. "You know what's going to happen tomorrow, that you'll be sold."

Sold.

"Yes," she managed around the sudden knot in her throat. "Yes, Master."

"There's something I feel I need to tell you." He stopped and glanced at her, then started walking again. "Your new master will know everything about you."

That's impossible. No one knows everything about another person. "Because he'll see the training videos?"

"In part. How do you feel about that?"

Master had never asked her such a question. Maybe, like many other things, she should keep her opinion to herself, but something about the breezy evening and full moon was opening her up. "There's nothing I can do about it."

"Those videos will demonstrate your strengths and weaknesses, your sexual responsiveness and how you handle pain. Your new master will know which buttons to push."

"I don't want him to. It scares me."

"What does?"

Could they go on walking until the Carnal facility was far behind them and only the moon and stars lit their way? "Being so vulnerable and exposed."

He wrapped his hand around her arm closest to him and turned her so they were face to face. A familiar hot charge lanced through her and the body she believed was sexually spent came to life. "Your owner will know more than how you react to being restrained."

Acutely aware of Master's collar against her flesh, she

acknowledged him. Her fingers burned with the need to touch this man.

"I'll give your file to whoever buys you. I don't have a choice. Record keeping is required of every trainer."

He didn't have a choice. Did that mean he didn't want to pass certain things on to whoever bought her? "What's in it?" He wouldn't have told her what he had if he didn't intend to be honest, would he?

Instead of responding, he let her go and started walking again. She took a couple of steps then stopped. No matter that her heart pounded painfully, she couldn't remain silent.

"Master, what are we doing out here?"

He turned and faced her. The sound of the surf gliding over sand eased her a little. Every time she saw him she was struck anew by his hard masculinity. Tonight the moon seemed to be bringing out another side to him. He was still all physical power, but that had been muted a little by the soft light. This man had become her world, not just her captor and trainer but the essence of everything she now was.

"I pride myself on being honest," he said. "If nothing else I owe you that on this, our last night together."

Don't say that.

"Your new owner will know everything you told me about the impact your father's death had on you."

"My guilt?" she whispered. "He'll know..."

"That isn't the only thing, of course, but maybe it's the most important." He returned to her and rested his all-controlling hands on her shoulders. The oversized garment did nothing to lessen the impact. "Maybe it won't matter to him. It's possible he won't give a damn about you as a human being but—"

"He'll know how much being a jockey meant to me," she blurted. *Damn these tears!* "He'll use that against me, bring me down with reminders of everything I've lost. Everything you've taken from me."

There. She'd said it. Thrown blame at him. Regardless of the consequences, she wasn't sorry.

"You're right." His chest rose and fell. "I kept after you until you had no choice but to tell me what you did. I know what it's like to be passionate about something, which means I have a damn good idea what no longer being able to race has done to you."

He was hitting her with too much. She couldn't deal with it all. Angry and confused, she jerked free. For one wild second she imagined herself running, then reality circled her. "You don't know everything. Almost, but not everything."

"Does it have to do with your father?"

Surprise warred with the sexual need she felt every time she was close to Master. If she answered honestly, would he pass that information onto whoever bought her? A month ago she wouldn't have said anything because Master hadn't touched her heart. That, like everything else, had changed.

"Yes," she said. "How did you —?"

"You aren't the only one with parents."

Had he mentioned his parents before? If he had, it had only been superficially. Now, maybe, he was ready to go deeper. The thought of what he might be willing to share with her thrilled her. However, she didn't know how to make that happen. Maybe if she opened up, he'd do the same.

And if not —

"Losing Dad impacted me in so many ways." Much as she wanted to go on looking into his eyes, she couldn't and get the words out. "Every time I started to care about a man I got scared. I was afraid something would happen to him or he'd leave me. It was easier to walk away than to live in fear."

"It wasn't just easier, Marina. You took the coward's way out."

Marina. He'd called her by her name. "Do you think I wanted to be like that? Of course I didn't, but…"

His hands again settled on her shoulders. For reasons she didn't comprehend, she stepped toward him and rested the side of her head against his chest. When was the last time she'd willingly turned herself over to someone else? Maybe years.

"I didn't expect that," he said.

"Neither did I," she admitted.

"Please don't hold back."

I'm trying not to. "I think I was finally getting strong enough to take a chance on a relationship before—before *this* happened. I'd finally figured out that my inability to commit revolved around how I'd lost my parent."

"Self-analysis can be a bitch."

No matter how wonderful his arms around her felt, she had to study his expression, so she pulled back a little. Her hands went to his waist. How strong he was.

"You said something about knowing what I've gone through because— Were you talking about your relationship with your parents?"

He shook his head then clenched his teeth. "I don't have to say anything." Soft as his voice was, she suspected he was talking more to himself than her. "Only we'll never see each other again, so what the hell does it matter?"

'Never see each other again'. Her throat tightened so she couldn't respond.

"But it does," he muttered. "You didn't tell any of the men in your life that you're afraid you'd lose them like you did your father, did you?"

"No." Maybe she should add that she'd ended things before the relationships could become more than casual, but she wanted this to be about him, not her.

"We all keep secrets. Every damn one of us does."

Just this morning she'd believed she understood what existed between Master and her, but that had changed in the past few minutes. Maybe that's why she reached up so she could caress his cheeks. Stubble abraded her fingertips.

"What's your secret?" she asked.

"Mine," he muttered. "Yeah, it's come to that."

"I hope it has."

After a moment he nodded. "I considered myself a jock almost from the time I learned how to walk. I still think of myself as one. Jocks are defined by what they are on the outside."

"Maybe, particularly in football, because they have to be so tough."

He looked surprised. "That's right. What brought you to that conclusion?"

Smiling came easily. "I'm in—I was in a sport that calls for a lot of toughness."

"Yeah," he muttered. "You're right and I needed the reminder. No one ever asked me why I was so aggressive. They didn't care as long as I did my job."

His football career was behind him, which should have meant he never had to talk about this, but maybe he was trying to explain why he'd been drawn to slave training. As for why he'd chosen her— "Why were you aggressive?"

When he stepped back and faced the ocean, memories of what had taken place between them nearly distracted her, but she forced herself to remain in the present. To wait for him to speak.

"Several reasons all rolled into one." He jammed his hands into his back pockets. "My old man's a total opposite from yours. He should have never had children. He sure as hell didn't want me. It was my fault for being born that so many of his dreams didn't come true."

Pain tore at her, but as much as she longed to comfort him, she sensed he needed time with his thoughts.

Word by word, he detailed what growing up with a distant and unloving father had been like. His mother had been so passive she wondered if the woman had been emotionally abused. At the same time, she blamed Tray's mother for staying with a man who'd barely acknowledged his son's existence. His father had shown some affection for the girl who'd been born when Tray was five but had continued to treat Tray like a non-entity.

"I tried so damn hard to get him to notice me — at least I did, until I finally got it through my thick head that nothing I did would make a difference."

"You hoped excelling at football would —"

"Yeah." Shaking his head again, he faced her. The moon touched his features with silver highlights. "Coaches and other players' fathers applauded my performances. I got written up in the local paper and girls — I never had to worry about attention from the opposite sex."

She didn't want to hear that, not that she hadn't already concluded he must have been quite the stud.

"Did he ever watch your games?"

"Oh yeah. He'd come with his drinking buddies and get all puffed up if I did well, but if he ever hugged me after a game I don't remember."

She studied Tray's face, looking for a hint of tears, and when they didn't appear she realized how successful he'd been at locking his emotions away. One thing she was certain of, he still felt the pain. Otherwise they wouldn't be having this conversation.

His father had been a trucker, which meant his job had kept him on the road for extended periods. His parents had gotten married when his mother was a high school junior and pregnant with Tray. They hadn't had a honeymoon, and his mother had moved into the one-bedroom apartment over a grocery store his father rented. She'd dropped out of school and, although she'd eventually gotten her GED, she had few employable skills and worked sporadically at minimum wage jobs. Once Tray had become a pro, he'd told his mother that if she wanted to get a divorce, he'd buy her a house, but although he knew she'd been tempted, his parents were still married and living in the place he'd paid for. Tray's guess was that she was afraid to be on her own. He wasn't sure what kept his dad in the marriage, maybe inertia.

"My being able to pay cash for a new three-bedroom place

was more than my old man could wrap his mind around. He kept asking how much I was making—questions he wouldn't have had to ask if he'd been involved with my career."

"It's so hard to believe," she said. "You've done something only a very few people are able to, something I'd think would make any father proud."

"Yeah." He studied the sand. "His old man was the same way and Grandma wasn't much better. Affection wasn't in their DNA. My old man was a product of his upbringing, just like me."

"You're wrong," she blurted. Despite her vow to give him the space he needed, she grabbed his hands and rested them against her breasts. A familiar fire seared her. "You aren't cold or remote."

"Aren't I? Most of the guys I played with are married and here I am."

"You didn't meet the right woman." Why was she saying this when it might not be true? "Eventually you'll—"

"And then what? I'll tell her where my paycheck comes from, invite her to watch me at work?"

Of course not. Maybe he'd become a slave trainer as a way of keeping a barrier between himself and a prospective wife. The only women he'd get close to for the rest of his life were like her, sex slaves.

"Aren't you going to say anything?" he asked. "Tell me I didn't turn out to be a bastard like the sperm donor."

He was asking too much of her, maybe deliberately forcing emotional distance between them. She should let him do what he wanted so she could face tomorrow having made a break with the man who'd molded her in ways she hadn't believed were possible. They were done.

Except—

"Answer me something," she said as she returned his hands to his sides and back-stepped. When she was sure she had his full attention, she pulled the jersey over her head and dropped it to the sand. "Can you imagine your father handling a woman the way you did me? Getting close?"

His attention remained on her face. "No. Absolutely not."

"What do you think he'd say if he knew what you're doing now?"

"Who the hell knows or cares? It isn't as if I'm going to tell him. Look, don't get me wrong. He loved bragging about his son the pro football player. He just never sat down with me and asked what the life was like. What *I'm* like."

"I don't know you either." *And it's too late for that to happen.*

"You know more about my upbringing than anyone else. While I'm at it I might as well explain about something. When I was twelve, we moved near a horse stable. My little sister always wanted me to take her there."

"She was horse crazy?"

"Was she ever. At first I wanted nothing to do with them. One day I was there when a foal was born. I got to touch it when it was only a few hours old. Its mother — she was so gentle. They both liked being groomed. The more I worked with them, the more comfortable I became."

"Handled right they're affectionate."

"Yeah. We never had pets because my mother was allergic. I didn't know getting close to an animal would — I learned to ride, not as well as you do. There's something about a horse's warm breath and seeing trust in their eyes."

You needed to connect with something alive. She tried to blink away her tears. Then, as one trickled down her cheek, she decided to hand him as much as he'd just given her. To remember more than just her body.

"Trust is a beautiful thing," she said. "You understand so much about me. And not just about this." She flattened her hands over her breasts with their hard nipples. "Like the impact my parents' deaths had on me." She swallowed. "My dreams."

Watching his eyes narrow and his jaw tighten, she knew she'd said the one thing she shouldn't have. Every nerve in her body screamed at her to run, but she couldn't let things end between them like that.

Her tears dried as she leaned over and picked up the jersey, intending to put it back on. "I was wrong," she whispered.

"About what? Thinking you could seduce me?"

"No." The truth was, she couldn't say what had prompted her to do what she had. It wasn't as if her body hadn't belonged to him for the past month—or that she'd wanted more than what they had. "I know better."

"Come here." He jabbed a finger at the ground.

Yes, Master, she nearly said, but the need to have tonight end on a different note kept her quiet. Head high, she took the two steps. The hot buzzing throughout her kicked up a notch.

He slid a finger through the ring in her collar and forced her head up. His gesture was familiar, but it felt different tonight. Maybe it was the setting, maybe knowing they'd never see each other again. She no longer cared about tomorrow, let alone the rest of her life. Even the words she'd thrown at him that had ended their rare openness didn't matter.

There was only him, his body and the way hers responded to it, the slave skin she'd allowed to be slipped over her.

"Do what you have to in order to survive," he muttered. "Be proud of what you've become. Please your master and find pleasure in the act."

His words rolled off her. She saw his mouth move and the darkness in his eyes—that was all.

"I'm not going to say I'm sorry for what I put you through. Even if I meant it, it won't change reality."

"No, it won't."

He let go of the ring, but she remained where she was. Several seconds ticked by while she stood before the man she considered her master. Maybe she should tell him how she felt, but there might be another way. One they'd both remember. She dropped the top he'd given her.

When she rose onto her toes, the sand beneath her feet

shifted. What had started out as a graceful movement turned awkward. She grabbed his shoulders to keep from pitching forward. Off-balance, she leaned into him. Her breasts flattened against his chest. She started to laugh. His erection stabbed her. She fell silent.

Master was looking down at her with his mouth slightly parted. In the background, the sea endlessly churned and unseen seagulls cried out.

They kissed. Hard and long. Lips parted and tongues engaged in an erotic dance that had her moaning low in her throat. Her nipples throbbed and sex juices dribbled. Heedless to the strain in her calves and arms, she held on with all her strength. She locked her hands around his neck. He cupped her buttocks and all but lifted her off her feet. *This isn't happening,* she tried to tell herself. She wasn't clinging to and kissing the man who'd turned her into a sex slave, and yet she was.

Because she needed the memory.

When he stopped supporting her, she sank back down. Her breasts were no longer sealed to him, but the hard burning sensation in them remained, as did the pulsing in her sex. His cock had been a hard, insistent length, and his lips looked as bruised as hers felt. She had no words, no explanation for what had just happened.

"One last time," he said and unzipped his jeans. She didn't wait for him to pull out his cock before yanking off the shorts he'd given her and kicking them away.

He claimed her space with a single step, closed his hands around her waist and lifted her. Understanding, she spread her legs and arched her pelvis toward him. He entered her in a long, fluid invasion. She wrapped her legs around him and pressed her heels into his buttocks. She gripped his shoulders. Powerful as he was, he easily kept her in place as he began bucking against her.

She was riding him, being ridden by him, two bodies joined in an ancient and primitive ritual. No words. Nothing approaching an explanation, because there wasn't any. He barely existed beyond body and cock and she didn't care that he was using her, if he was.

They were ending. Their chapter over. Finishing on a high and hot note.

She swore she heard her body snap and crackle as she had sex with the man who'd locked a collar around her neck. Thoughts came to life but kept dying.

"Damn you."

"No," she shot back. "Damn you."

He made a sound that could have been a chuckle or a curse. Instead of trying to determine which it was, she stared up at stars she hadn't seen for so long. A burning, building sensation exploded from her core and encompassed her. She started flying, drowning, rising and falling, screaming. Head back and nails digging into his shoulders, she lost herself in the moon and a long and thunderous climax. Holding her hard against him, he repeatedly slammed into her. Came.

When he had nothing more to give and her legs lacked the strength to go on gripping him, he eased her to the ground. They stood near but not touching for what might have been a full minute, each sucking in air. Then, saying nothing, he picked up her discarded clothes and pointed in the direction they'd come from.

Their time together was over.

Chapter Twenty-Five

"I'm scared," the slave standing next to Marina whispered. "And excited. I think I know who's going to buy me. If it's him, I couldn't ask for more."

Instead of pointing out that freedom should have been that *more*, Marina only nodded. It was early afternoon and she, along with a half-dozen other slaves, were in a small, windowless room with two doors. One at a time they'd been led through the small door and were now waiting for the larger to open. Unlike yesterday when they'd been pawed over, except for their collars and the leashes dangling from them, they were free. They were naked, of course. Judging by the multitude of aromas, every slave had taken care with their personal hygiene. They even had makeup on.

Of course. A slave needed to look as attractive and valuable as possible in order to garner a high price. She'd thought Master would oversee her preparations, but she hadn't seen him since he'd returned her to her room last night. Instead, the middle-aged woman she'd heard referred to as Mrs. Johnson had brought cosmetics and a curling iron and ordered Marina not to move as she painted her face and added waves to her straight hair.

She tried not to wonder whether Master would watch today's proceedings, but the question surfaced nonetheless. The ordeal ahead of her would be easier without him. At the same time, she couldn't imagine having him out of her life.

"What about you?" the slave who'd been talking asked. "Did any of the potential buyers appeal to you?"

A month ago she would never have believed she'd hear

such a question. Now it was part of her reality.

"None. I can't do this. I can't."

The other slave patted her on the shoulder. "You don't have a choice. Make the best of it. That's what I'm going to do. Besides, there are benefits."

She didn't need to see the slave run her hand between her legs to know what she was getting at. However, despite her conditioning, sex wouldn't be enough for her.

Someday, somehow, she'd escape.

The large door opened and two men dressed all in black walked in. She'd thought the slaves would be forced to wear restraints like last night, but the men's hands were empty.

"Here's the drill," the shorter one said. "You're going to enter the auction room one at a time. This" — he grabbed the leash of the woman closest to him — "hopefully will be for show. Conduct yourselves as proud Carnal graduates."

That was all the men were going to say? No lectures or warnings? As they left with the woman whose leash the one had picked up, she acknowledged that nothing more had been needed. Regardless of how long each woman had been in training, she wouldn't be here if she wasn't deemed ready. Instead of wondering what was going on in the next room, her thoughts kept returning to a simple fact. Master had changed her from a woman who took self-determination for granted into one who'd made her peace with her new reality. Much as she'd regret never seeing him again, and she would, her body craved this sensual journey. She'd become a slave, not just to a man but to her primal needs as well.

One after another, the other women departed with the black-clad handlers until just two of them remained. By then her companion was shaking, so she'd sat cross-legged on the cement floor to keep from falling. The woman's sex was in plain view, further proof of what the time at Carnal had accomplished.

As for Marina, she just wanted today to be over.

The other woman pulled her knees against her when the door opened. However, instead of the two men, Master filled the space.

Master!

"Come with me." He indicated the door she'd come through so long ago.

Barely believing this was happening, she obeyed, her feet making faint slapping sounds and the leash dangling between her breasts. She wasn't dreaming, hadn't imagined this was happening. Master led the way down the corridor. Instead of returning her to her room, however, he turned left. Despite her confusion, she vowed to wait for him to explain. Last night he'd said many things. Today was different—but in how many ways?

He opened yet another door then stepped aside so she could go in first. This was his space. Several football posters had been taped to the walls. More telling, it smelled like him. This was where he slept, dreamed, thought.

Leaving the door open, he walked over to the closet, opened it and took out a familiar blue blouse. She'd worn it a few times when she'd had occasion to look professional. The white slacks he dropped on his queen-size bed were nearly new, since she usually had to worry about keeping her clothes clean. He indicated the oversized gym bag next to the slacks. "Some of your underwear's in there. Go on. Put them on."

Silent, she reached into the bag and pulled out items she'd nearly forgotten about. She selected white panties and a bra and dressed. Her mind all but shut down. All she knew was she wasn't ready for that to change.

Underwear was unfamiliar. Once she'd slipped into the slacks, however, she could hardly wait to cover herself with the protection the blouse provided. She'd always felt more feminine when she wore this outfit, but never as much as she did today.

"There," he said. "Done and done." Staring at her, he ran his hand through his hair. "You look amazing."

He'd never seen her with makeup on and with her hair styled, but she sensed that wasn't all he was talking about. Something about being dressed resurrected her sense of confidence. Ignoring the collar and leash that remained as a reminder of everything she'd been through, she sat on the side of Master's bed. His scent eased around and through her.

He sat in a recliner. "You aren't going to ask are you? You're waiting for me to explain."

"Yes."

"Good." He nodded. "Damn good. This is the spark I saw in you last night, the one the past month couldn't kill."

"Are you sorry? Maybe you wanted a mouse, not a woman?"

"No. I'd never want—look, I don't want to draw this out. There's been a change of plans. Obviously you aren't going to be sold."

Because someone had already bought her?

No, she wouldn't ask. He'd brought her here. Let him face the consequences of his action. All she had to do was face a future without her first owner.

He sighed. "I don't know what's so hard about saying this except— Marina, I spent the morning buying your freedom."

Her heart slammed against her chest wall. "You..."

"I don't think this has ever been done at Carnal. At least I'm guessing that's why it took so long."

"I'm free?"

He shrugged. "Did you hear what I said? I paid what a new owner would."

"Then you— I belong to you?"

"It's more complicated than that."

What did he mean? Unable to remain seated, she got up and stumbled over to his window. A wide stretch of ocean and shore took her back to last night.

"You get to see this whenever you want?" she asked, with her back to him.

"Yes. Every time I do, I'm reminded of how much you'd enjoy seeing it. Look at me, please."

Please? She'd nearly forgotten the word existed. He'd swiveled the chair around so he was facing her.

"I don't belong here," he said. "I kept telling myself the feeling would go away, that the job's perks would make up for the downside, but it didn't."

"What downside?"

"If you don't know the answer it's because I did a damn good job of keeping what I was going through to myself. Feeling as if I owned you, knowing I could do whatever I wanted to your body—those are powerful emotions." He shrugged. "There's a Dom inside me all right. I don't blame you for thinking of me as a bastard. Even if I wanted to, there's nothing I can do about that."

"You aren't a bastard," she whispered. "Maybe that's how I saw you at first, but no longer."

He didn't look convinced. "There are some things I need you to understand. I'm making as much of a break from Carnal as possible, which should mean I've also severed my ties with you, but you can't just walk out of here."

Her heart beat painfully.

"In exchange for taking you out of the system, I had to promise to make sure you don't tell the cops." He nodded at the bed. "Sit down. The explanation is going to take a while."

She sank onto the bed. After maneuvering the chair back around, he explained that Carnal's influence reached into areas of law enforcement, the legal system, politicians. Not all police, lawyers, and politicians were dirty, but key figures were Carnal customers.

"This is how it was explained to me," he finished. "If you want to go on living, keep a low profile. Otherwise you'll disappear. Not *might* but *will*."

Her throat dried. "I understand."

"Do you?" He leaned forward. "You're going to be watched."

"Can—" She had to refill her lungs before she could continue. "Will I be able to go back to being a jockey?"

He massaged his temples with such force she was afraid he'd hurt himself. "That's what you want?"

She tried to picture herself on horseback but couldn't get the image to form. Maybe later, once she'd had time to process what she'd just heard. Was she free or wasn't she? Maybe she belonged to him.

"I don't know what I want. It's been so long since that's been an option. What about going back to my place?"

"And risk running into those who told Carnal about you? Not a good idea."

"Then my place..."

"Will have to be sold. Yes."

Yes. What a simple word, one that could be full of layers. "Why are you doing this?"

His already sober expression became even more so. "I thought you'd ask how I accomplished what I did."

"It cost you a lot of money."

Watching him nod opened something up inside her. Until now, she'd been trying to wrap her mind around one word at a time, but that no longer mattered as much as what was going on inside him. From the first time she'd seen him, she'd thought of little except his impact on her. That hadn't left much time for trying to crawl inside his mind, or wanting to.

Learning about his father's impact on the man he'd become and his love of horses had taken her into his world, but it hadn't been enough.

After planting her legs under her, she pushed herself upright. Walking over to him both frightened and thrilled her. When she was close enough to touch him, she sank to her knees before him and placed her hands on his thighs.

"Why?" she repeated.

He stiffened but didn't push her hands off him. "It came down to a matter of facing myself in the mirror. Controlling you, making you do and experience whatever I wanted—

let's just say I have dominant tendencies. I want to be the one in charge, to call the shots, but that's a hell of a way to go through life. I'd been a bastard long enough."

"You aren't—"

"Look, I'm not going to apologize for what I did. I got off on a lot of it."

She resisted ducking her head. "Just as I got off being submissive to you."

"You really—"

"Yes."

He pressed his fingers against his upper lip. "Yes? I didn't expect you to say that. Maybe that's because I've been hung up on myself."

Determined to keep the conversation going, she nodded. "In what way?"

"More than I want to think about. Self-analysis can be damn time-consuming. Example, last night when I was telling you about my parents, something occurred to me. My old man kept my mother under his thumb. I swore I'd never be like him, but I was."

"No," she insisted. "What goes on between your parents is hardly the same as—you know. She could have left."

"Maybe once. Not anymore. She has no spirit."

"Does he beat her?"

"No, but he puts her down. He says he's stuck driving trucks until they put him in a grave because she can't support herself." He sighed. "That's how he saw me, a burden."

Say what you're thinking. "So you're separating both of us from Carnal because you needed to prove to yourself that our relationship isn't like your parents'?"

He closed his eyes. "That's deep. Look, I've gone back and forth about this, weighing what I want against what you deserve." He took a long breath. "Maybe what I need to say is that, after today, we don't have a relationship."

Is that what I want? "What about you?" Talking made her throat hurt. "What are you going to do?"

"You care? Yeah, you do or you wouldn't have asked. Maybe I'll buy some acreage and put horses that need homes on it."

If he could do that, he was even wealthier than she'd thought. "That's beautiful," she whispered. When he opened his eyes, she lowered her head. "I had a similar dream for after I retired from racing. I just lacked the funds."

"Not *had*," he muttered. "It doesn't have to be past tense. Just because I bought your way out of Carnal doesn't mean you belong to me. I've had enough of being selfish. It's your turn."

"My turn for what?"

"Doing what you want, at least as much as possible." His lungs slowly expanded. "I've said this before but have to again. I'd like nothing better than to keep that collar on you, but it isn't my decision to make."

"You're saying it's mine?"

He stared at her neck. "Yeah. Like I said, I've been a bastard long enough."

"You're not. Damn it, you aren't." Giving weight to her outburst, she spread his legs and kissed the mound she knew so well. Administering to his cock, even with denim between them, transported her back into a familiar world.

"Do you know what you're doing?" he asked.

She responded by kissing his cock again. Shuddering, he stretched his fingers over her head. Today might never completely sort itself out for her, but she didn't care. Being with Tray had changed her, taken her out of the cocoon she'd been living in for long and shown her what it meant to be a sexual creature. She reveled in her new self. Couldn't imagine living without it.

Didn't want to live without him.

"Master, I—"

He silenced her with a hand over her mouth. "Don't call me that anymore."

"What if I want to?"

"You can't—"

"Yes, I can and do. Master, you said a part of you still wants your collar around my neck, right?"

"Yeah." He drew out the word. "Damn it, I do."

She fingered the familiar band. "Don't remove it, please. And don't send me away."

"Send? I'm handing you freedom."

The clothes that had felt so strange when she'd put them on had no place in this conversation, but she couldn't think how to change that until she'd said and done what she needed to. She pressed the palm of her right hand against his cock. He was becoming even more erect.

"This is what I want," she told him. "You in my world."

He groaned. "You'd better mean it, because I want you so damn bad I might not be able to stop."

"Don't stop, Master, please."

Less than a minute later they lay side by side on his luxurious bed. He'd removed her clothes, although ripped was a more accurate description. She'd pulled off his shirt, then stood with her head bowed and the leash brushing her naked body while he'd finished stripping himself.

"There's a lot to be decided," he said as he moved her arms out to her sides. Her legs were already bent and spread, her sex gaping in invitation. "Plans we have to make."

"Yes, Master." Much as she needed to embrace him, she'd remain splayed for his pleasure. In her submission, she'd find joy.

He crouched on his knees between her legs and drew her onto his thighs. When her pussy was inches from his erection, he lightly ran a blunt fingernail over her labia. A long moan erupted from her throat.

"You'll race," he said. "That's your domain and what brings you joy."

"Yes, Master."

"At night you'll come to me. Do what I tell you to."

He hadn't said it, but she understood. The master–slave relationship would continue only as long as they both wanted it.

When he pushed her onto him, she tightened her inner muscles around the man she'd given her body and more to.

Plans and decisions could wait.

This fever couldn't.

More books from
Totally Bound Publishing

When wannabe sub Jennifer Berklee calls him Master and begs him to flog her, PI Logan Powell knows all his military training won't be enough to keep his jaded heart safe.

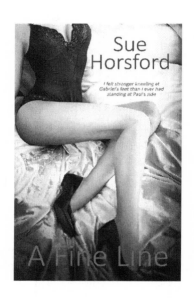

No one would understand that my submission empowered me, that I felt stronger kneeling at Gabriel's feet than I ever had standing at Paul's side.

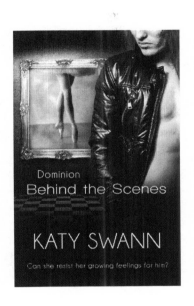

Dominion
Behind the Scenes

KATY SWANN

Can she resist her growing feelings for him?

He's a famous rock star…and an irresistible Dom. She might be his submissive but she'll be damned if she's going to let him think he's better than her.

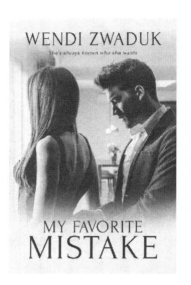

She's always known who she wanted. Now she needs to find the strength to make him see they're more than a mistake.

About the Author

Vonna Harper

What prompts a mild-mannered mostly law abiding woman to write erotica and erotic romance, a lot revolving around BDSM and capture/bondage? Is it the complex issue of taking or giving up control?

Vonna Harper doesn't know and she has given up trying to find the answer. It's enough that many readers are drawn to what some call the dark side. All she asks is that readers understand she writes fiction--a brand of fiction she finds fascinating.

Vonna has lost count of the number of books, novellas, and short stories she's written. What she has no doubt of, it's a hell of a ride.

Vonna Harper loves to hear from readers. You can find contact information, website details and an author profile page at https://www.totallybound.com/

TOTALLY
BOUND

Home of Erotic Romance